FALMORA
A NOVELLA
AND SIX STORIES

DEBRA LITTON

CONTENTS

FALMORA

CHARACTERS & GLOSSARY

Bandun – (Dun, the elder; father of Fendun)
Neenah – (Nah, Bandun's mate; mother of Fendun)
Fendun – (Dun, the younger)
Farliam – (Liam, father of Andreno)
Andreno – (Reno, brother-friend of Fendun)
Tanéha – (Néha, future mate of Andreno)
Angara – (Gara, father of Allia1onae)
Fanáh – (Anáh, mother of Allia1onae)
Allia1ónae – (Lónae, future mate of Fendun)
Jardán – (Dan, father of Tunendan)
Myraynah – (Raynah, mother of Tunendan)
Tunendan – (Dan, infant; future leader of Irelmen)
Havar – (the evil one)

aruh: hello/greetings
is't: is it
larn'd: learned
on'y: only
th': the
thá: you/your
thar: there
thé: they/their
un: I/me/my
whar: where

CHAPTER I
GLADE OF FALMORA

*I*t is little known that an ancient race survives deep in the forest Falmora. Being only twice the size of a red squirrel, they inhabit the small caves and hollow trees quite handily. These are not what some call leprechauns, but are real people, grown small over eons. They are careful to disassociate themselves from what they call the human people. They call themselves the Irelmen. The Irelmen have lovely dark skin and even darker hair of black or shades of brown. In contrast, their eyes are light blue, or sometimes green. A rare atavism occurs usually once or twice in a generation when an Irelman is born with light hair — said to be common among the ancients, of the time of Havar.

Among Irelmen it is common for mates to have only one child in their lifetime. It's not due to their desire for only one child, but to the fact that their fertility is extremely low. In the rare instance of a twin birth a great celebration is held which lasts a week.

The naming of an Irel baby is a solemn and wonderful thing. Because Irelmen do not have inherited family names, the one name they are given at birth is chosen with great care. In order to be sanctioned, the name must have at least two syllables. And it is customary to use only the last one or two syllables of each person's name — for, after their initial birth ceremony, it is forbidden to call out anyone's entire name.

The Irelmen believe that their full name will be called by the Great One and so are always intently listening for the sound of their full name. This listening must never be interrupted by everyday usage of names. So it is that Bandun is known as Dun and Neenah as Nah, and so, for each. The fact that many people have the same last syllables on their name *creates no problem, for each person's name is pronounced with a unique intonation.*

A fresh fog swirled through the deep forest of Falmora, leaving pockets of clear evening air around the rock-lined pools of natural springs. The evening's muted half-light delineated the trees, gnarled and twisted, grown up through rocky ground. Tiny brown birds made their last searching circles around the tree trunks before sunset.

In the safety of the big oak, Neenah sighed and wiped her hands on her cooking smock. The food was ready and the sun was disappearing—she wanted Bandun to return. She worried about him when he went hunting squirrel. It was a danger he was getting too old for. The squirrels were always a danger especially now in the fall when they wanted to move right in with you and steal your stores. At that thought Neenah waddled down the root steps to the cellar to check on the stores for the twelfth time. In the dark damp bottoms she began to count, when suddenly she heard shuffles above. She gasped aloud and remembered the food set out on the table—*Arrl, an' un weapon left leanin' at th' stove,* she thought in dismay. As quietly as possible she stumped up the root stairs, and, keeping well against one wall, she peeked out of the cellar opening into the kitchen.

Bandun stood, hands on hips, in the middle of the room. Behind him at either side of the entry lay two dead squirrels. When he saw Neenah peek in from the cellar, Bandun began to rock on his feet from heel to toe in pleasure.

"Arrl!" exclaimed Neenah. "An' look at th' size o' 'em! Thé be half as big as thá. An' thá brung 'em both in alone?"

"Ha Hah! Thé be'd not much for th' strongest Irelman alive!" Bandun slapped his chest in enthusiasm.

"Be thé full dead?" asked Neenah as she inched sideways toward the two huge red-furred bodies.

"Doubt un would bring in any but full-dead?" He scowled at her careless question and Neenah's lower lip puckered out as she looked down in shame.

"Let it pass," Bandun's voice gentled. "'Tis not a night for lookin' down. What 'ave thá cooked for th' celebrate, Nah?"

Neenah cheered at the mention of the food. She waddled quickly to the table and showed her dishes proudly. "One that's thá fav'rite, salamander heads set well in a lovely orange jell. An' to go with, acorn bread with roly-polies laced in for crunch."

Bandun's eyes gleamed. "Thá be a good mate, Nah."

Neenah blushed. "Ah, Dun. Thá deserves better, but thá gets all th' love from th' one in hand."

They hunched over the small carved table and ate several servings from the special shell plates Neenah had brought from her mother's house as a gift on her mating day. They ate in silence with the cooking fire lighting their faces. Both cast glances at the bodies by the door, but neither let thoughts of the morrow's work interfere with the evening's serenity. Neenah would be glad for the new skins but she dreaded the burying of the carcasses. Her thoughts questioned again the necessity for abstaining from squirrel meat, but she knew better than to speak her doubts—the laws of Havar were many and strict and not questioned.

Finally sated, Neenah got up to bring a candle to the table. As she set it down and eased back to sitting, Bandun leaned forward and whispered, "Un saw one that thá once knowed today."

Neenah gasped and looked around her in fear. Bandun glanced nervously at the entryway, then continued, "Un did not speak nor show un presence. T'were on'y a glimpse un had."

Neenah nodded in understanding. Her face reflected deep sorrow. She looked away into the fire. "How was it that one looked?" she asked softly.

Bandun's heart thumped heavy and choked his words. "One...one looked to be in some good health, though sorrowed one seemed. Alone, an' not bright on th' world."

A silence fell. Neenah thought back to the time that brought this ache to their lives. She thought of her son Fendun, the one they could not speak of with his given name.

One month ago, in the glade of Falmora, there was a party to celebrate a birth. The end-of-summer's warmth still clung to the forest.

The young mother Myraynah held her tiny round child in her arms and slowly revolved in the midst of all the Irelmen so each could see. Her mate, Jardán, repeated the child's full name aloud three times for all to hear. They called him Tunendan—henceforth to be called only Dan, like his father.

Since this was not a twin birth the celebration only lasted one day and one night. A great length of vine rope was suspended from one edge tree to another so that it spanned the width of the glade. All the men had contests and placed bets on who could travel the length of the rope, hanging by their hands and moving in a hand-over-hand motion. As the day progressed and the rope stretched closer to the ground the children were able to reach it. In unison they swung it back and forth until they made grand sweeping swings across the glade. Everyone ducked and yelled in mock terror as the line of giggling children swept through the middle of the celebration.

The women gathered wild grasses and fragrant herbs. The excess plants they put in a pile and lay the new baby Tunendan on the soft nest to sleep. The reserve plants were given to Myraynah along with personal recipes for medicines and ointments. The women had many tales of child-rearing to exchange and they had much advice for Myraynah about the proper care of a baby.

The men held wrestling contests in the warm sun and the women cooked and giggled. Everyone held the new baby in arms of love by turns—and each had a large quantity of sweet wild violet wine, often in disregard for whose turn it was at the tap.

Neenah pushed forward to get her own refill and then found a grassy spot to sit. She gazed happily into her large gourd of lavender-colored wine and remembered the long ago birth ceremony of her own baby Fendun. His celebration had been held as a twin birth because another child, Andreno, had been born only a day later than Fendun. And so it was that the Irelmen had a wonderful excuse to combine the births into a weeklong celebration. And so it was that Dun, the young, and Reno, were treated like brothers from the first and grew to be as brothers. Each spent every hour in the company of the other during their youth.

Viewed together, the two young Irel boys were a superficial contrast in looks and habits. Fendun grew muscled and powerful, while Andreno was long-limbed and slender.

All Irelmen are hunters. Fendun spent his days practicing and honing his skills. Andreno learned only enough to protect himself, then turned his efforts to creating new designs for dishes and carvings for furniture. This made Andreno odd among the Irelmen, though most were fair minded and saw the worth and beauty of his designs. However, one thing set Andreno apart and caused an uneasiness among the Irelmen. Andreno's hair was a rare light color.

Andreno was a very young boy when his mother died. One day while gathering berries in the forest, she was crushed badly by a falling tree limb. Although disease is unknown among the Irelmen, sometimes an injury becomes infected or an accident causes such trauma that nothing can be done for the sufferer. Andreno's father, Farliam, could not withstand the loss of his mate. After the accident he ceased to interact with others and would not talk to anyone. Liam took care of only the rudimentary needs of his son Andreno, and young Andreno drew all companionship from Dun and the community of Falmora.

As young men, though not as constantly together, Fendun and Andreno always knew each other's activities. It was therefore not unusual that Fendun, losing sight of Andreno, went in search of his brother-friend during the celebration of Tunendan's birth.

"Reno! Whar thá art?"

Neenah heard his shouts coming closer to the edge of trees where she sat. She watched Bandun among the small group in the middle of the glade cheering on the wrestlers. She felt glad to know where both her men were and to see the happiness of all the people. She heard Fendun's calls directly behind her now, in the woods. And then her breath stopped as she heard the full scream—"*Andreno!*"

All the party hushed as the name echoed through the glade.

No one moved and they looked from face to face in confusion.

Fendun walked out of the forest behind Neenah. Bandun saw him and began to walk to him. As he moved, the others followed Bandun's direction and all spotted Fendun. Neenah turned around and looked in time to see Fendun shake his head at Bandun. Neenah gave a short cry. Fendun walked to her and laid his hand on her shoulder. He was crying. Neenah reached out to him, but he turned and ran back into the forest. As his son disappeared into the underbrush, Bandun clenched his eyes tight and murmured, "May all evil fall free from thá."

At first it was imagined that Andreno must have died. For what other cause could there be for Fendun to break the taboo?

In silent accord the Irelmen moved toward the spot in the trees where Fendun had emerged, intent on discovering whatever sad scene had prompted Fendun's outcry. As the front of the group neared the trees, Andreno stepped out into the glade, head downcast. A common gasp flew from the crowd but none stepped forward to question him. Whatever had happened was between Fendun and Andreno. By ancient decree Fendun was exiled and only Andreno could speak the words of forgiveness that would allow him to return. No one could speak of Fendun by name until he had been formally absolved.

CHAPTER 2
FENDUN'S EXILE

Fendun ran stumbling through the undergrowth. He tripped on an exposed root and lay pounding his fist and weeping aloud. After his crying subsided he lay very still, listening. He knew there would be no followers, yet he hoped somehow a voice behind him would say, *Return now, Dun. 'Tis all a fiendish mistake.* He lay a long time listening until the sky grew dark. With a sudden fear he realized he must find a shelter for the night. Drawing himself up to a weary stand, he walked without direction and finally spent the night in a semi-hollow at the base of a large tree.

The first days of his exile were the easiest, for Fendun wandered in a stunned grief with a blank mind. When hunger and the chill of coming winter forced him to attend to his survival, he searched for a permanent lodge and found a small cave with a natural spring at the opening. The site was a mere two day's walk from the glade of Falmora, and, although still in the forest proper, it might have been a foreign land. For Fendun lived outside the warmth of Irelman society. His solitude was total—no word, smile, nor friendly gesture comforted him. His existence was not softened by the comfort of animal companionship—there is no animal small enough nor of docile nature that an Irelman can safely take it into his affections.

Fendun gathered just what was necessary to survive. Only when his stomach was intensely painful with hunger would he scavenge for whatever food was close to his cave. Many days he ate only grubs and slugs skewered on a stick and smoked over his fire. Occasionally he found a few edible seeds or mushrooms.

While gathering firewood, he had chanced upon a straight and hard wood staff that would serve as a spear. Inside the cave he squatted and rubbed one end of the staff against the stone floor to sharpen it, then held the tip over the dying fire coals to harden the point.

The winds were blowing colder every day. Fendun huddled in the back of the cave. He knew he should gather stores for the coming winter. He would need squirrel skins for protection against the cold. Yet he sat gazing into the fire, turning his spear slowly in his hands. His thoughts went no further than the scene he had witnessed by the glade.

As his spirit sank, so did his will. He did not attempt to hunt and eventually he ceased to search for grubs. His daily effort was to crawl to the cave opening, drink from the spring and add a few sticks to the shrinking fire. Within a few days he lay curled by the fire's coals, shivering and unable to move. He closed his eyes, ready to sleep without waking.

Small mice, scurrying to gather winter stores, darted ever closer to where Fendun lay. He watched them through the dim fall light, but made no move to try to capture them. He thought of the great red squirrels and their danger and his heart would race for a few minutes, but still he made no move.

Drifting in and out of a weakened sleep, with his ear lying next to the forest floor, Fendun began to hear noise of a large creature moving through the forest. He would hold his breath when a rustling occurred, but he remained curled by the fire embers. On the third day of his laying in despair, Fendun heard a careful pressing of the forest floor leaves. A large creature was slowly creeping behind his head. His instinct was to jump up and twirl on the unknown, but he only clenched his fist tightly on his spear and closed his eyes.

The sound was stealthy, considered—not the sudden scuttle of a squirrel, not a furred creature. Fendun thought suddenly, *Thé be come for un! Un be forgiven now!* He slowly rose sideways on his hands and was just turning his head to look behind when a great crashing sound swerved his eyes to the front. Down through the high tree limbs, bouncing on outstretched branches and bringing dead wood with it, a great red squirrel fell and thumped to the ground so near to the fire that small sparks flew out at the impact. Despite his hunger weakness, Fendun lurched to his feet. He had seen squirrels fallen stunned after a bad judgement in leaping the high branches. He knew he must act quickly or face a deathly fight. With a surge of strength he lifted his spear above his head and plunged it into the squirrel's chest. The effort brought him falling down on top of the animal and he lay panting against the rough fur.

As he slowly gained his breath, Fendun sensed something was not right. He rolled to a sitting position beside the body and stared at it. Where his spear had entered, there was only a small trickle of blood, not the usual great spurt of red from a fatal wound. He cautiously crawled to the animal's head. The eyes were glazed in death and protruding from the back of the neck was a small slender spear, like a child's toy.

"'Tis been killed afore!" Fendun exclaimed and his own voice shocked him alive. *By another!*—his thoughts screamed and at the thought he suddenly remembered the noise at his back, before the squirrel fell. His head jerked to the spot beyond the fire. There was no sign of another, but on the ground lay a bundle of skins.

A flush of excitement flowed through Fendun—*'Tis Reno. Thá be come!* But abruptly he knew that if he were truly forgiven, there would be no need of hiding and sneaking in the woods. The offerings were left in silence because he was left in silence. Not forgiven, but remembered.

The weight of his aloneness crashed around him just as the heavy squirrel had crashed to earth. He felt again the confusion and hurt of the event that had caused his exile. But, looking at the mysterious gifts that could start his winter survival, he determined to endure and to seek out the reasons behind his changed life course.

"Un be returned, Reno," he pledged. "Thá must tell th' words that bring un back. An' then un be knowin' th' reason un had to leave."

As the dark began to seep through the forest, Fendun struggled to drag the squirrel carcass into the cave. He built up the fire with the dead wood the squirrel had knocked down and finally settled exhausted at the cave mouth and drew the skin bundle toward him. He slowly unrolled the hides. It was a winter sleeping hide finely sewn into a large pouch, the hair side turned in. And inside, a smaller softly-tanned carrying pouch held a large assortment of foods: cracked walnuts and acorns, dried berries and mushrooms, a small pouch full of roasted roly-polies and three small baked loaves of acorn bread.

Though his hunger ached, Fendun forced himself to eat slowly. Between scoops of spring water he chewed mouthfuls of the bread until he'd consumed a whole loaf. He carefully wrapped the remaining food in the pouch and pushed it far to the back of the cave. Then, with his stomach aching from the unaccustomed amount of food, he wrapped himself in the warm sleeping pouch and slept.

CHAPTER 3
ANDRENO'S ANGUISH

The glade of Falmora held no comfort for Andreno, for it brought all the memories of his life back to him, and his life memories were the same as his stricken brother Fendun. Even so, at night, Reno came to the glade and sat at the edge between the trees and grass. He thought of what he must do to bring Fendun back and his soul would sink at the certain consequences to himself.

An Irelman does not boldly lie, for it has always been proven that the truth eventually comes to tell its tale to all. However, an Irelman will often take a long time to explain events or his own actions, in order to stave off the bluntness of truth and soften its impact when it finally comes to tell.

Andreno thought the terrible past scene through his mind again. He had heard the noise of approach behind him, and hurried to conceal his secret. He was not quick enough. Though the carcass was partly covered with leaves, he had dragged the thing to the opening of a hidden thicket and the massive head and shoulders lay exposed when Fendun stepped through the trees.

Even as Fendun shrieked his full name, Andreno motioned to Tanéha and she ran from them into the woods.

Tanéha...Andreno had told only Tanéha some of his secret. Though Fendun was like his brother, Tanéha seemed an extension of his being—a twin half. She was like most Irelwomen in appearance, dark hair and green eyes, but in her actions she was different. She knew things before Andreno said them aloud and she accepted his thoughts without thinking him strange. However, as events lay unfolded and not resolved, even Tanéha wondered at Reno's behavior.

During the day Andreno kept to himself. Most often he was hunting or preparing stores for winter, but never in company with another Irelman. When duties such as tanning skins or repairing weapons required staying by his fire, Andreno would work quietly and alone, head downcast and not acknowledging anyone's presence.

The Irelmen did not understand. What had occurred to cause this simultaneous break of taboo and rift between brother-friends? And why was Andreno so reluctant to pronounce the forgiveness? And, perhaps most disturbing of all, what caused Andreno to forsake all community among his people who relied on communication and trust? Unease grew as Irelmen remembered Andreno's sporadic but lengthy absences from the glade in the last year. There were times when he had stayed away two and three days, returning not with food, but only brooding hours of contemplation. Then, after Fendun's exile, Andreno's wandering stopped. The Irelmen began to avoid this young man of such odd behavior, and his rare light hair, so different from their own, became a symbol and eventually was suspected as a cause of his aberration.

Like Fendun, Andreno was an outcast facing the coming cold winter alone. In the evenings, as he sat by the glade's edge, Andreno would hear the soft steps of Tanéha. Instead of a greeting, he acknowledged her presence with an even lower hanging of his head. He did not shun her completely, for he sat very still and did not shrug away her touch when she laid her hand on his.

"Reno, what be th' thoughts that keep thá hidden so? Do ye turn thá face ev'n from un?" Tanéha leaned low to try to search Andreno's face but she could not capture his eyes. After a time, she would hang her own head and sit silent beside him. Her soft dark hair fell around her face and concealed her tears. When she finally rose to leave, Andreno's face too was wet with tears.

To Bandun, Andreno was the one link to his son. Forbidden from direct contact with Fendun, Bandun hoped for some clue to this misery, some answer and path to resolution. He stalked Andreno.

Though Andreno no longer looked directly at any Irelman, he felt the fierce questioning gaze of Bandun follow him. Often in the woods hunting or gathering nuts, Andreno would catch a glimpse of Bandun squatting low under heavy brush, staring, watching—still and barely contained, his strong brown legs crouched and ready to spring. Bandun watched Andreno as prey. His thoughts ran through a recital: *What hold keeps thá forgivin'? How dare ye be silent? Truth'll come, Reno. Un be in wait o' it!*

Neenah too kept a vigil, but not one so apparent. She noted the actions of Andreno when they coincided with her own movements around the glade, but more than Andreno, she carefully watched Tanéha. Instinctively, Neenah felt a certain knowledge in the younger woman and she knew the confidences between Andreno and Tanéha must include part of the secret reasons which forced her son away.

As the winter stores mounted up within the tree cellars and caves, the Irelmen began to have time for talk and small gatherings. Women grouped around the springs while they sewed special warm coverings for feet and hands. They talked softly and laughed at the Irel babies playing by the cold water. The men squatted around small fires in the glade sharpening spears, making and repairing utensils or furniture. They told tales of past hunts and planned new ones. Disputes over details of the tales brought good-natured outbursts of challenge or laughter and the noise broke in bursts over the quiet clearing.

Bandun was explaining his double kill of red squirrels. For a lone hunt, it was a rare tale, but the telling swelled with Bandun's pride.

"It were th' one good spear un had on'y," he told. "An' as soon as piercin' th' heart o' th' one, un be turned to slash th' double comin' behind un!" Bandun jumped to his feet to mime the actions for the listeners and stood hands on hips waiting their approval.

One Irelman looked puzzled and spoke out, "How be it thá freed th' spear from th' one in time for th' pierce o' th' other?"

Another joined in, "Aye, Dun, what spear will not hold tight in th' red beast after 'e is struck down?"

All listeners leaned a little forward and Bandun rubbed his nose. His eyes rolled upward to help his memory—"Uhhn...it comes clear now." He looked around at each face in wonder as the sudden memory came. "It be that un carry th' short spear hanged at th' side. Th' short spear is th' one that speared th' other."

"Ahh," the group exhaled in understanding. All heads nodded in appeasement and they settled back to work. Bandun went back to his whittling on a new spear but his eyes looked over the heads of the group at a solitary figure. Alone, but within hearing, Andreno sat at the forest edge. He was intent on carving an eating bowl. For an instant his eyes flickered up to meet Bandun's and then dropped again in a confused expression.

Are sorrowed? thought Bandun. And then in anger, his thoughts screamed, *Alone beyond th' glade, an' th' coldness comin'! What chance is't thá be givin' un son?*

Bandun could no longer sit and peacefully work. "Arrl!" he pushed to his feet and stalked away toward his tree, leaving his weapons. No one questioned. They knew full well his anger and its cause.

From the far side of the glade three young boys came chasing into the open. A few men glanced up at them and returned to tasks. One boy shrieked out and another screamed, "Squirrels! Thé comin'!"

The men chuckled at the game. But Andreno, watching the young runners, saw terror. He jumped to his feet. The carved bowl clattered on a rock as he raced toward the group of men Bandun had just left. The group stared shocked at Andreno as he rushed past, stooping to grab Bandun's half-finished spear.

Bandun swirled around at the noise and saw Andreno sweep up his spear, running. "Ayee!" he screamed and rushed at Andreno to revenge this new insult.

Suddenly crashing the underbrush and scattering dry leaves, in frantic side-to-side dashes, two red squirrels raced into the glade, their high-pitched "Chirrups!" shattering the air.

For a moment the animals stopped erect on their haunches, spiky bushed tails flipping rapidly up and down. All men grabbed for their weapons. Bandun stopped in surprise. He pivoted and ran toward the fire for his spears.

Andreno, running now with the spear raised high for throwing, reached the nearest squirrel and thrust the weapon in one great heave. The point cut into the animal's neck and it screeched, thrashing the ground and clawing at the wound.

The second squirrel swirled in retreat back toward the trees just as a group of frightened women emerged from the same point. In terror, it swirled again and sprinted, then leaped at Andreno. Just as the other hunters reached the spot, the squirrel knocked Andreno to the ground. As a dozen spears thrust into it, the squirrel's sharp teeth slivered Andreno's leg.

Andreno screamed a single pain-shriek and then was silent as the Irelmen rolled the bloodied carcass away from him. They grouped around him and Bandun pushed his way in to stoop down by Andreno.

Andreno lay still, contracted in pain. His face was very pale. His eyes met Bandun's. "Un borrow'd thá spear..." He looked for a moment as if he would smile and then his face contorted in pain.

Bandun reached to touch him and then abruptly stood and stepped back, his face set hard in the thought: *An' who is't be thar if such 'appens to Dun?* Without a word he turned and pushed through the crowd to help skin the squirrels.

Neenah and the other women gathered around Andreno, but each hesitated to give aid to one who had shown such lack of compassion. Then Tanéha, forcing her way to the front, knelt beside Andreno and took his hand. She looked at his gushing wound and knew it must be cleaned. Her eyes looked up at the faces around her.

"Please," she pleaded, "Carry Reno to th' water."

The Irel women broke their vacant stares and each moved to action. Two rushed for a skin to carry Andreno. Others ran to scoop gourds of water to splash on the wound. A few knelt down too and murmured comfort and encouragement.

Neenah stood uncertain. She watched Bandun working over the killed squirrels, his movements sharp with anger. Then she looked down at the fallen Andreno, his eyes glazed in agony. A sharp pain came to Neenah's chest and tears pushed into her eyes. She too thought of her own son's danger in the forest and she anguished at her inability to help him. But this suffering one, brother-friend of Dun, was now in danger too.

As a skin was brought, Neenah softly reached to help lay Andreno onto it and grasped an edge as she and the others carried him to the springs.

The women rolled Andreno to his side so that his leg lay in the small stream and the cold water swirled over and around the wound. Tanéha held his head in her lap while the others cut away the hides of his leg covering and brushed gently on his wounds with evergreen branches while the stream carried away a diffusion of blood.

Tanéha watched the red blood spurt from the wound, turn to pink in the water and disappear as the stream carried it away. Andreno's strength seemed to seep away with it. In panic, she quickly slipped a rolled skin bundle under Andreno's head and stepped into the stream. She squatted quickly, her skirts swirling in the water around her. She grabbed Andreno's leg and pressed her wet skirts to the wound with her palms.

Andreno groaned and she darted a glance at his face but kept pushing at the leg.

For long minutes no one spoke and the Irel women watched in pity at the young woman shivering in the water desperately covering the wound of the one she loved, as if defying its existence. Then, gradually, the watchers noticed the water was no longer red, and they murmured to each other pointing at the clear stream.

"'Tis stoppin' th' blood!" said one.

Tanéha began to sob aloud but pressed her hands tight to the wound.

Neenah spoke out so suddenly the others jumped: "Thar be not a place for this one, no mother to care for 'im. Thá help to carry 'im to un tree."

Neenah stooped to lift Andreno, and the others, their eyes wide in surprise, helped carry him to Bandun's tree. Tanéha would not give up her hold and clambered beside in her wet skirts, pressing the wounded leg.

Up the inside root steps to the inner chambers, Neenah led the group to Fendun's sleeping room. The women laid Andreno carefully on the sleeping skins and quietly backed away and out—back to the glade and their common work.

Tanéha bent in stupor over Andreno's wound, grasping his leg. Neenah placed her hands on Tanéha's shoulders and said, "'Tis good now. Thá will loose thá hold." Tanéha cautiously released her grip, peeling her skirt away from the wound, then scrambled to her feet and rushed out before Neenah could speak.

With a heavy sigh Neenah glanced at Andreno's still face and pulled a skin over to warm him. Then she hurried to the cooking stove to heat water. As the water came to a boil, Neenah jumped at the sound of running feet and Tanéha stood with her arms full of comfrey leaves. Neenah nodded in approval. Together they crushed the leaves in a bowl and added enough boiling water to form a paste. When it was cooled, they carried the poultice into Andreno and Tanéha carefully patted the green mixture to his wound while Neenah looked for a strip of skin to wrap around the treated leg.

When they had done all they could for Andreno, Neenah pushed a stool close and guided Tanéha to sit by Andreno's side. Then she quietly returned to the kitchen and sat at the table to wait for Bandun.

What will Bandun say on this matter? she wondered.

She thumped her fist on the table and declared, "Thá mayn't be pleased, but thá canno' say tis wrong!" Then her face looked doubtful and she brooded silently as she awaited Bandun's return.

CHAPTER 4
ADAPTATION

Fendun's strength returned slowly with the help of the small food supply. It took him two days to bury the squirrel's carcass and even then it was not buried deep or far away as it should be, but Fendun left it and began in urgent purpose to prepare for winter.

He staked out the squirrel's skin and smoked it over the fire for a hasty preservation. When it was taut, he hung it just inside over the cave mouth to keep out the wind.

He searched the forest close to the cave and found a few berries and roots to store. By chance he found a small comb of honey and stole it from the bees in the evening hours. There were still a few grubs and mushrooms to gather in the damp spots under logs and rocks, but Fendun knew these few gathered supplies were not enough to last the winter. He began to plan a desperate effort: with some small luck he might be able to raid the winter cache of a squirrel and carry away enough nuts to last through the worst months. An hour's walk from his cave, two young squirrels held a cache in the roots of an old fallen tree. Fendun watched the animals and gauged their habits. Each afternoon they slept—but always next to the fallen tree or on the cache itself. However, in the mornings, they spent an hour or more chasing and playing through the forest and Fendun could reach their stores unobserved. He was able to steal only once a day, but using the now empty pouch, he could carry many nuts away at one time.

Within a week, the back of his cave was piled as high as his waist with stolen walnuts and chestnuts. On the first day of the second week, Fendun sneaked quietly back for a final raid on the squirrels. Just as he reached the underbrush near their fallen tree, two squirrels sprinted out of the nut cache chattering and screeching. Fendun recognized the one chasing, but knew the other must be an intruder. As he watched from his hiding place, Fendun saw the squirrels lock in a vicious fight. Their bodies squirmed somehow locked together in violent bites until suddenly one lay silent in the leaves. Attracted by the noise, a third squirrel scuttered down a tree trunk and just as it reached the ground, Fendun heard a soft *thump* and the squirrel tumbled somersaulting onto the ground and lay twitching, a small wound rhythmically gushing blood behind the shoulder.

Fendun gasped and stood up out of his camouflage. The remaining squirrel, seeing the sudden movement, rushed crookedly toward him, stumbling from its fight. In a reactive motion, still too surprised to feel fear, Fendun thrust his spear directly into the squirrel's chest and circled away from its dying thrashes.

Panting, Fendun forgot caution and ran to the squirrel that had tumbled from the tree trunk. Sticking from its wound was the same type of spear-like weapon that had killed the animal at his own camp. Fendun wrenched the weapon out of the wound and examined it. The tip was very sharp and fire-hardened like a throwing spear, but this was small and lightweight. At the blunt end there were whittled notches in the wood with bird feathers extending from each. It was not a weapon used by any Irelman he knew. And how was such a light spear thrust deep enough to kill, without standing very near the prey? And there was no one near when the squirrel was hit.

Fendun suddenly jerked his head to look in all directions around him. There was nothing. The small birds had not yet taken up their song again in the trees; something must be among them. A cold fear grabbed Fendun and he darted into the underbrush. Squatting hidden and breathing rapidly, he watched for some sign of movement around the scene of death.

After a long wait, Fendun began to calm and feel bolder. He chastised himself for the time wasted. Cautiously, he crept up to the nearest squirrel and hoisted its limp body onto his shoulders. He made his way back to his cave as fast as his burden allowed. When he had made two trips and one squirrel remained, he thought of leaving it, but the winter would be long and cold and the skins would be his only protection.

Exhausted, he returned to the fallen tree and lifted the last squirrel to his back. A sudden breeze rustled the dry leaves in the tops of the trees. Fendun shivered and glanced around him once again. Then, even with the tired drag on his muscles, his legs somehow hurried from there.

Fendun immediately cleaned the carcass and set it aside, wrapped the skin around the brains of its host to cause a soft and pliable tan. This one he would wear against the cold. Even as he worked, he felt a watching presence.

The other two skins he tanned hard and smooth like the battle shields he'd heard of in the stories. Sewn tightly together with sinew and stretched over the back wall of the cave, they hid his stores. The deep brown coloring seemed to tint the air within the chamber with a somber copper fog. As the air grew colder, Fendun gradually moved his fire closer to the cave mouth. When the flames danced and cast light into the cave, the skins seemed viable, as if some great petrified beast turned outside-in on itself. Fendun held his breath and felt the slow breath of a larger being surround him.

CHAPTER 5
ENCOUNTER

A presence seemed close to him often now. In his solitude, Fendun's senses sharpened and he was aware of sounds and sights not acknowledged before. With his food supply secured, his thoughts had time to drift. He often brooded on Andreno and the cause of his actions; but more immediately he wondered about the strange small spears and what creature had used them.

What if there were spirits? Fendun shuddered. Since the time of Havar, such thoughts were forbidden. Havar declared there are only Irelmen, and the Great One, living in the forest with the small beasts and animals. No one should cause fright and confusion by suggesting that some other manner of life existed. If it were so, the old ones would know. For when an Irelman grows very old he will walk into the forest toward the west and stay there far from the noise and confusion of the people, to devote all his time to listening for his full name to be called. If there were other beings in the forest, the old ones would have returned to warn the Irelmen.

Fendun's thoughts raced: *But what if th' beings prevent th' old ones return? What if th' beings be violent? What if thar be an edge to th' forest, an' a place not like is known? Would th' beings take th' old ones to that place?*

His thoughts stabbed at Fendun and deeply disturbed him. He spoke aloud to dispense them. "Ha! It be not so!" He embraced any physical movement to keep his thoughts at bay and exhaust himself. For hours he searched for deadwood for his fire or gourds to use as containers. He fashioned elaborately insulated foot coverings from bark and fur and skin. And he honed more spears than one Irelman would need.

One night, unable to sleep, Fendun roamed into the forest. Most of the leaves had fallen from the trees and the white, silent moonlight filled all but the heavily overgrown space. He was able to find his way quite easily.

The cold air burned in his nose and his breath puffed frozen clouds around his face. All the forest seemed to await the winter's grip. The birds were abrupt and brief in their songs and the squirrels did not often leave their nests.

Fendun was drawn back to the fallen tree. He sat close to the spot and leaned his back against a tree trunk. *If thar be spirits*, he thought, *thé be not violent to Dun.* He nervously fingered the small spear weapon secured at his waist and wondered if it was possible to see a spirit and if so, what would one look like?

Abruptly, a silent shadow moved overhead blocking the moonlight. Instinctively, Fendun looked up and at the same time heard the whoosh of great wings. He held his breath and sat very still. He had only seen the night bird twice before, when hunting after dark, and had watched it kill quietly and swiftly, scooping mice into its angled claws. He knew even the slightest movement would mean death. His eyes followed the low flight of the huge floating predator until finally it glided silently away and out of view.

Fendun let out his breath in a long sigh and lowered his head — then froze again. There in front of him, only a few paces away stood a being, a man. He stood still and looked at Fendun, but the moonlight shone behind and obscured his features. He was smaller than an adult Irelman, and flowing from his head, falling silver-white around his shoulders and to his waist, was a mass of hair not common to an Irelman's wrapped coil. The man made no sound, but began to walk toward Fendun.

"What manner o' being be thá?" whispered Fendun.

At that moment the great night bird's screech filled the air to herald a kill and the startled being ran forth toward Fendun. Fendun raised an arm across his chest to ward off attach and scrambled to his feet. He saw in a glance that the man held no weapon, yet advanced headlong. Terrified, Fendun fled crashing through the underbrush, away from the ethereal white-haired one.

Even in his panic Fendun thought to lead the man away from his cave. Taking a wide circular path, he moved urgently, but cautiously, aware of the need for silence. After making a complete arc around the cave, he crept to within a few yards of his camp and hid low under an evergreen copse. He waited, listening. No sound came from the forest and nothing moved in the glow of moonlight. Fendun waited for several hours in his hiding place. As the moonlight faded to darkness, he crept carefully back to his cave and crouched inside, ready with his many honed spears.

As the winter-grey dawn arrived, Fendun began to tell himself it was a dream.

Un did not hear 'im comin', he thought, *'e be not truly thar*. His head nodded and his muscles relaxed as he convinced himself. Then he thought of the day of the squirrel kill and saw again the squirrel rolling down the tree trunk. *Un did not hear 'im afore*, he thought, *an' the small spear be real enough*.

He struggled to his feet and groggily tried to decide his next move. He lifted an edge of the skin flap from the cave mouth and peered out. The morning was without sound or wind. Every bush and tree seemed to hold very still in wait.

Fendun felt weak from lack of sleep and he was beginning to be hungry. He glanced at his fire and saw that it needed more wood. The morning light was bright now. It dispelled the murky light of night and the anxieties that floated with it. Fendun shrugged his shoulders and began to prepare food as on every morning. Along with nuts and berries, he took a handful of myrica bark from one of his storage gourds and heated some water for tea to keep him alert.

As he squatted by the fire and sipped the strong fragrant tea, he suddenly realized how foolish his actions had been, for the man/spirit knew of the cave—he had killed the first squirrel at Fendun's campfire.

"Be it were 'e an' not another," he said aloud.

At that moment the small man stepped out of the forest and stood again silently regarding Fendun. Fendun jumped to his feet, spilling his tea into the fire with a loud hiss. He stooped for his spear and the stranger spoke.

"Hold!" The voice was soft but commanding.

The single word stopped Fendun and he straightened to face the talking spirit. It held no weapon and he took courage from that. In the bright morning sun, the man's full hair was now golden. His face was delicate and looked more fair than manly. He walked slowly toward Fendun with no threatening gestures. As he came close, Fendun saw that he had deep blue eyes and a strange look of amusement on his face.

As Fendun watched, still frozen in his actions, the man crouched very slowly and picked up the dropped drinking gourd. As he stood and slowly extended the cup to Fendun, his outer furs fell loose and Fendun saw the soft-tanned inner skins covered full breasts.

"Ah!" Fendun cried in shock. He stepped backwards and lost his balance. As he hit the ground, he saw the strange visitor briefly frown and then throw back her head and laugh.

"Thá be no man!" blurted Fendun.

"An' thá be not fine mannered," she laughed.

Fendun sat on the ground confounded. He looked at the solid human flesh before him. "Thá be a true being," he said. "Be thá Irelman?"

She gave him a strange look and considered the question for a long moment. Then she nodded once and answered, "Aye."

Fendun soared at the answer and lost all apprehension. The sound of another's voice after the silence of the last months filled him with warmth and relief. He jumped to his feet. "Whar come thá?"

Ignoring the question, she lifted the drinking gourd to her face and sniffed the container. Again she extended the cup toward Fendun and said, "Thá have myrica? Un be thirsty."

Fendun was silenced by her boldness and her blunt dismissal of his question. But he hurried to get more bark from his stores. As he worked to heat water, she watched him in silence. He nodded to her to sit by the fire, and they both sat close to the warmth, sipping silently.

Without warning, the woman stood and said, "Allialóne."

Then she abruptly sat down and looked at Fendun expectantly. At first, Fendun did not understand. Then he realized she had given him her full name. With a pounding heart he rose and said, "Fendun."

"Dun," she repeated in the accepted form.

Fendun nodded and sat again. "How are thá called?" he asked, not knowing how her name should be shortened.

"Lónae," she said.

Again they were silent. Fendun repeated her name to himself and a thousand questions came to him. From where had she come, this strange woman who said she was Irelman yet had never been in Falmora Glade? Why was she dressed as a man, in leggings instead of skirts, and her hair flowing free instead of bound and braided? Did she own the small spears? What did she want of him?

CHAPTER 6
BROTHER-SON OF TREL

Bandun had returned to the tree at dusk with a bit of sewing sinew and a set of claws as his measure from the squirrel kills. As he climbed the vines to the upper entrance, Neenah hurried to set out his food and his washing water.

"Aruh, Nah," Bandun greeted her quietly and handed her his pack. Neenah loosened the sinews and set them to soak in evergreen oil while Bandun silently washed his hands and face and sat to eat.

As she joined him at the table, Neenah searched for words to tell him of her actions. He must not sleep the night, not knowing of Andreno under his own shelter. She cleared her throat and tried to begin.

"It be a day for mem'ry," she said.

"Mmmph," Bandun nodded and chewed.

"Thá was not hurt—tis glad'ning," she continued.

Bandun nodded again and lifted one eyebrow in question at her nervous manner.

"Thar be some can use th' new skins," Neenah stated.

Bandun stopped eating and looked directly at Neenah. "What is't thá will say? Be no need to speak around th' matter o' Reno—how is't thá say 'e be? Thá have knowing?"

Neenah gave a tentative smile and her eyes darted as she searched for the right words. "Aye, 'e be cared for, but heavy stricken," she answered.

Bandun nodded in approval. Before he could speak, Neenah continued, "'Tis in need o' great constant care. With no mate to care, no mother. An' with father not in 'is wits, 'e be alone with…"

"Nah!" Bandun stopped her gruffly. "Know un well what manner life be Reno's. What be thá purpose in this tellin'?"

Neenah looked anxious and her eyes involuntarily glanced toward Fendun's sleeping room. Bandun followed her gaze then looked back at her in disbelief. "Arl !" he yelled and pushed up from the table, stomping across to Fendun's doorway. Neenah hurried behind him and screamed as he jerked the skin covers from Andreno's body.

Tanéha gasped and instinctively wrapped her arms across Reno's head and chest.

"Be damned!" roared Bandun.

"No!" screamed Neenah. Tears fell onto her anguished face and she clutched at Bandun's arms. Bandun glared at her. She did not lower her eyes, but looked directly back at his and pleaded, "'E has no shelter…has no mother, no one. A son alone."

Bandun stopped and considered these words. He looked at Reno's pale still body and Tanéha's frightened but defiant face. He looked at Neenah's tortured eyes and his muscles seemed to sag. Slowly he spoke and tears welled to his eyes.

"A son o' Irelmen," he agreed, and quietly left the room.

In the first days of his injury, Andreno drifted in and out of consciousness, alternately burning then shivering with a cold that was more than the early winter chill. Tanéha stayed by his side bathing him in cool water and keeping a poultice on his wound. She would not venture to other parts of the tree when Bandun was there. She would gratefully accept the broths and food morsels prepared by Neenah, first feeding Andreno and then eating some of what remained.

Bandun was unusually silent. He came in only to eat and sleep. Each day before he left he would silently look into Fendun's room and watch Andreno for signs of healing. He felt discomfort at stalking one afflicted, but his need to hear the words of forgiveness spoken overshadowed all else.

Tanéha too began to wait for Andreno's words. Beyond the care she had for him, her thinking was not squelched, and she tried to reason why he withheld his forgiveness. What he had done was not good and both Fendun and she had witnessed it. However, the deed was surely forgivable, if only Reno confessed. But still, he held quiet. There must be something more, beyond the mere confession; there must be something in the explanation of the deed that held him in quandary. What could it be that held his tongue and kept his brother in exile?

During the hours that Andreno slept, Tanéha tried to fit the events of Reno's behavior together with some logic and cause. Reno had told her that he had dug some buried squirrel carcasses. When she had questioned why, he said only: "Th' meat be taken. Not by chewin' o' animals—taken by cut!"

The knowledge had frightened her but it only seemed to anger Andreno. He began his secret absences, always returning by night and sometimes carrying strange objects which he kept hidden, far from the glade. When Tanéha protested the dangers of his lone absences, Andreno replied there were far greater dangers than squirrels to face.

"An' tis no' knowin' full truth what keeps a danger."

One morning before dawn, Andreno woke without fever. His body ached with long hours of lying down and his wounded leg felt numb. He had had moments lucid enough in the last few days to recognize where he was, but now his mind worked clearly and for the first time in many days he felt his will return. In the hour before light, Andreno thought over all the things he had discovered and the implications of those discoveries. He thought of the care he had received from ones he held in agony by his reticence; and he thought of his brother, outcast and far away from all who cared.

By the time a pale light entered the room, Andreno was no longer confused about what he should do. For a moment he watched Tanéha sleeping just a few paces from him, and he thought of the dangers his actions would surely bring to her and all Irelmen. Then, as he watched his breath float out onto the chill air, he realized with horror how far into winter the fall had come and thoughts raced to Fendun—perhaps unsheltered. Andreno raised himself on shaking elbows and called out:

"Néha! Whar be Dun? Dun shall know!"

CHAPTER 7
HAVAR'S LEGACY

Without preliminary, as they sat by the morning fire, Lónae asked, "Thá know of th' people of Havar?"

"'Tis legend," answered Fendun, "all Irelmen be th' people of Havar.

"'Tis more than legend—tis truth. More, Havar divided the people," said Lónae.

"Aye, Havar an' th' warriors fought th' distant battle. None returned. Aught but few Irelmen be left."

"No! Thar be two peoples of Havar!" Lónae declared. "Th' ones in likeness o' Havar, an' th' dark ones be left at Falmora. Th' dark ones be left with false legend an' half o' what be true."

Fendun drew in his breath to protest, but in one movement Lónae stood and shrugged off her bulky outer furs, revealing an odd pouch hung at her back. Reaching her arm backward, she drew out one of several small spears and a curved stick with a taut line of sinew strung between the ends. She quickly crossed the two, held both by her cheek, and gave a sharp tug. Fendun heard a *swoosh* and followed Lónae's gaze to the trunk of a tree several yards away. There, the small spear stuck. Fendun sat speechless. Lónae retrieved her spear and handed it to him.

"'Tis one o' th' truths taken with Havar. Un be pledged to carry th' truth to Falmora an' return it to all Irelmen. For this un be exiled."

"From what place—exiled?" asked Fendun.

"Innismoor. Un will tell as un know't," answered Lónae.

And so Fendun heard the hidden half of the story of Havar. Havar lived in the lifetime right before the time of the old ones now listening in the forest. When all Irelmen lived in Falmora, Havar was well-known for his skill as a hunter and for his bravery. As a young man, he ranged farther than all others in his hunting, and his curiosity led him to explore widely, even when not hunting. Once he was absent for half the moon's cycle and all feared that he had died. But he returned and brought a frightening tale.

Havar told of a strange people, much like Irelmen in feature, but with wills bent toward violence and with unknown methods of wrecking destruction. He told the Irelmen that these people were moving toward Falmora and they must be ready to defend.

In a council meeting the decision was made not to let these strange people advance to Falmora. Instead, a party of men would be sent out in defense before the invaders even reached the forest or had a chance to discover the glade.

All men able to travel walked out of the forest Falmora. Blond haired and dark, with battle shields and spears, they left the forest as brothers in arms. A mere dozen young men stayed behind to hunt and to defend the glade. If anyone noticed that the men who stayed behind were dark, no one commented on it—then, or later.

Falmora waited anxious and hopeful for a messenger from Havar to tell them of the drift of battle; but none came. There was sporadic talk of sending a scout to follow, but no man could be spared and no woman would be sent alone in the forest and beyond.

Through the sad grip of winter and soft hope of spring, the people waited in quiet despair. Then, in late summer, a lone messenger arrived. He brought a tale of such despair and woe that the entire glade was plunged into mourning. All men had been killed. Havar and a small group had endured for several months by hiding and surprise attacks; but in the end, all were destroyed.

Havar had sent the messenger back to Falmora when it was obvious that all was lost. Before the final battle, Havar had a vision from the Great One. In the vision it was told how all men would perish at the hand of this Northern enemy. It was also told how the people of

Falmora could survive if they followed certain new laws. Those laws were: never to journey more than two days' distance from the forest Falmora; never again to eat the meat of squirrels, but bury the carcasses in plots marked with the special sign of Havar; and old ones must leave the glade permanently and travel West through the forest to listen for their names.

The people of Falmora were so frightened and despondent that any guidance was accepted without question. The new rules were instated and observed. However, a great despair overtook many of the women. Those who had lost mates, or who would never have a mate, found no meaning in their lives and one by one they walked deep into the forest—never to return. Of course, the women with children stayed on and lived as did the young women who were eventually mated to the few remaining Irelmen.

This is the story the Irelmen knew; but there was another side which Lónae knew. In the time of Havar's leaving, Lónae's father, Angara, was a young boy barely into adolescence. He was among those in the war party, though his main duties were to secure and carry supplies. As the warriors marched out of the forest Falmora and into unknown and frightening new land, Angara was as cautious as any soldier, but he also became alert to subtle shifts in the chain of Havar's command. During the marches by day, Angara observed that the dark Irelmen were the bearers of supplies, the hunters, the cooks; while the blond Irelmen were guards, scouts and weapons-masters. At night, the groupings of men around Havar's fire reflected firelight off light hair on heads bent close together in low-murmured conversations.

Even before they reached the destination of enemy camps, Angara was suspicious and uneasy. And one early morning, the warriors marched out onto the foggy moors, when the front men suddenly turned back and used their weapons on their darkhaired kinsmen. Angara did not hesitate to drop his burdens and run back toward the cover of hills.

Angara had no doubt about the result of the skirmish, for the dark Irelmen had effectively been disarmed over the course of the long march. In great fear, Angara fled back along the route they had covered. After running for two days, he realized that no one followed him and he began to wonder if he was the only survivor. He thought there might be others who escaped and he should join forces with them. Also, if the men of Havar were preparing to march back to Falmora, Angara should learn their plans in order to warn the glade.

Angara made a circuitous route back to the camp. He slept by day in heather-covered culverts and by night he spied on the warriors. The moors provided little cover to hide in, so Angara was never able to get close enough to hear conversations. However, at the end of the first week, he watched as the main body of men struck camp and moved onward toward the North. Angara's heart froze as he watched ten of the men linger behind, then start back toward him. Were they looking for him or did they plan to destroy those who remained in Falmora— or both?

Angara moved ahead of the men back toward the forest. His field supplies had run out, but he was able to forage enough grubs and plants to continue. Angara kept close enough to the group to know their movements, yet far enough ahead to run and warn the people in the glade when the time came.

When they were one day's advance into the forest, the men searched for shelters and formed a camp. Angara watched them for three days and was perplexed. They prepared their shelters and began gathering supplies and hunting, but they did not appear to be planning an attack. Around their fire at night, they joked and talked and went to sleep early. The winter was coming and Angara would need shelter, but he sensed that before he returned to Falmora, he should somehow learn the plans of this group of Havar's soldiers. If they had meant to return to Falmora to live, they would not have prepared for winter, but would have continued on to the glade.

Angara was sure they had a mission—but what was it?

One morning, Angara saw two of the men pack food and set off toward the glade. They took their weapons, but only their best spear, as any Irelman would. Angara tracked them through the forest. If this was an assassin team, he would cut them off before they ever reached the glade. But, he didn't have to. Not too far from the glade, they hid themselves in a well-concealed cave. Then a curious thing happened. They seemed to watch and wait. They concealed themselves in the brush and kept very still, as if hunting. *A trap!* thought Angara. But he was thoroughly confounded when he watched one of the Irelmen from the glade walk in sight one afternoon and neither of the hidden men made a move toward him.

What was the meaning? Not many days later, Angara got an answer.

A young woman walked through their site. She was not foraging, but seemed to have no purpose in her wandering. Angara sensed her hopelessness in the way she held her head downcast and walked without caution. When she was very near the hidden warriors, one of the men stepped out of hiding in front of her path. The woman gasped, and for an instant Angara read menace in the warrior and forgot his cover. He stood up in a rage and stepped forward. But the warrior smiled at the woman and put his finger to his lips to signal silence. In curious compliance, the woman followed the warrior's beckoning and they went on to the hidden cave. Angara quickly hid himself and tried to reason out this new action. Would the woman be held as hostage to force the men of the glade to give themselves up?

That same night, Angara watched as the warrior and the woman left the cave and moved out toward the North encampment of other warriors. Within two days a new warrior had arrived and the scene had repeated itself, with another Irelwoman led away by night. Angara suddenly realized: the men were returning for their women.

All this while, Angara had suppressed the personal anguish of his father's slaughter on the moors, and he had vaguely reasoned that his mother was safe in Falmora. But now he could not be sure. And, there was another in the glade, the young girl Fanáh, too young to be taken away as a mate—but perhaps not, for she was blond.

After weeks alone in extreme stress and physical deprivation, Angara lost rational thought. He had watched trusted men kill their own brothers. He had watched coveted women picked off and spirited away by night to the great moors of the North. He felt he must escape from all of the violent and senseless actions. Even the glade seemed unsafe to him. Then Angara too waited in concealment and captured the girl, Fanáh. By night he took her away—but, to the South, direction of banishment.

It took little to convince Fanáh of the truth of Angara's story, for her father had never returned and her mother had disappeared into the forest. It was harder to convince her that they must not return to Falmora, but she cared for Angara and she trusted him, so eventually she resigned to the idea.

Together they lived in the forest, unknown and away from all others. They grew up together and created a family and community in each other. After several years their daughter, Allialónae, was born.

Allialónae grew up in a lonely tangle of contradictions. From a very early age her mother told her tales of happy, peaceful life in company of other Irelmen in the glade, and her father told her of treachery and false kinships and the danger of life among others.

Her mother taught her traditional skills known by all Irelwomen; but both parents knew that her survival in the forest without the society of others depended on her learning all skills. So, from the first, Lónae was also taught to hunt and make weapons—and, she was allowed to wear leggings instead of skirts.

As Lónae matured she embraced parts of each of her parent's philosophies and formed her own unique beliefs. When she was 14 years old, her father disappeared; often gone for several weeks at a time, he would spy on both settlements of Irelmen, once bringing back the bow and arrow from the warriors in the North. Then, when Angara left and failed to return, Lónae set out alone to search for him. She made her way to the fringes of the Northern encampment and back again without finding any trace of her father.

For three years after, she took care of her grief-stricken mother. Fanáh finally could stand the solitude no longer and insisted they should go back to live with the Irelmen. Lónae resisted, for she had never lived among others and she was confused by her father's stories. In tenuous compromise, mother and daughter agreed to separate. Lónae accompanied Fanáh to the edge of the Northern encampment. Fanáh walked into the settlement of Innismoor to rejoin half of the people she knew from her childhood. The story she carried with her was of a vague wandering in the woods. She would not tell of her vanished mate, Angara, and her hope to find trace of him; nor would she tell of her daughter, Lónae.

Lónae promised to join Fanáh within a year; but first she must reconcile herself to a choice among the people of Falmora, the blond warriors of Innismoor, and her secluded life in the forest. Both women silently understood that Lónae carried her father's burning sense of injustice and her purpose lay in vindicating her dark-haired kinsmen of Falmora.

Lónae's isolation was broken by Fendun's exile to the forest. She had shadowed him from the beginning, and aided him when his will was broken. Finally, her curiosity and need for companionship overtook her fear and she had approached Fendun.

CHAPTER 8
SEPARATE REVELATIONS

Fendun sat very still after Lónae finished her story. So much of what he'd just heard was in conflict with what he had been taught as a child—and yet, all the events fit in sequence and made sense.

"Havar be still alive?" he asked suddenly.

"Thar be no knowin' o' that. Th' ones that follow'd be alive, an' th' ones that those come back for."

"Lead un to th' place thá call Innismoor!" Fendun demanded.

Lónae's eyes narrowed and she considered Fendun in silence. No one had ever spoken to her in such rude tone. She stood and stared at him with hands on her hips. Fendun felt uncomfortable with her reaction, then, angry.

"Well?" he asked, jumping up beside her.

Lónae snorted in disgust and began to pace toward the trees, then abruptly turned back and rushed at Fendun. "Thá canno' tell un what must be done! An' ev'n so—tis comin winter an' th' travel is long. We'd not make it in this time!"

Lónae glared at him.

Fendun sat down in surprise. He knew she was right, but her aggression still angered him. He glared back at her.

They stayed in silent standoff for several minutes.

Lónae retraced her walk to the trees and back, this time slowly, in thought. Fendun watched her graceful movement. The bag of small spears swayed softly on her back; her footsteps inaudible with practiced stealth. Fendun thought over what she had said and as Lónae approached the fire he nodded and said, "Aye," then asked, "Thá will show un Innismoor in th' spring?"

Lónae smiled and answered, "Aye, an' thá will lead un to Falmora!"

Fendun sadly shook his head and told her of the events that led to his exile. The recital of it all brought back the huge weight of sorrow and Fendun was morosely silent when he'd told the end.

Lónae did not understand all of what he told and she yearned to question him but knew she must wait. Without comment, she shrugged on her outer skins and walked into the woods. Fendun was so absorbed in his gloom he didn't consciously notice her until she was at the edge of the trees.

He looked up suddenly and called, "What?"

Lónae turned back to face him—"Un be return'd by darkness. Thar be not much to carry." Then she walked silently into the forest.

Fendun hunched further down by the fire, then sat bolt upright as he realized what she had said. Lónae intended to move her things to his cave! Fendun's thoughts were suddenly monopolized by a whole new set of anxieties.

When Andreno's voice rang out the early morning stillness, there was no need for Tanéha to seek Bandun. The call from Andreno was the one hope Bandun waited for. By the time Tanéha had reached Andreno's side and understood his meaning, Bandun was standing at the entry to the room. He was ruffled from sleep, but his eyes shone with eagerness and tears of relief.

Without a word Tanéha slipped out of the room and the two men finally faced each other alone.

"Thá must know all," said Andreno. "It be more than Dun to consider."

"Aye," said Bandun. He crouched eagerly by Andreno's side. Tanéha entered quietly with large steaming gourds full of tea for each.

She sat at Andreno's feet and Bandun started to protest. Then he saw the fevered indignation in Andreno's eyes, and he let the impropriety pass.

"Néha has knowin' o' this," Andreno said. Bandun looked surprised and uncomfortable, but he said nothing.

Andreno launched immediately into the explanations of his absences: the suspicions he had about the fair-haired Irelmen and their existence, and how all his investigations had proved his suspicions. He told of Innismoor and the new weapons he observed; and he told of the squirrel carcasses and what he had discovered in his exhumations.

"It be th' cut carcass that Dun watch'd un drag into open. An' Dun called out with no knowin' o' th' purpose." Andreno hung his head. "Thar be more knowin' that un could no' tell—un did not reason on th' whole o' it."

Urgency returned to Andreno, "Thar must be forgivin' for Dun. Th' winter be comin' deep!"

Bandun sat very still in thought. He now understood the reasons behind Andreno's actions. He thought of the reaction of the people of Falmora when they learned of the deceit of their kinsmen—and one more consideration of danger occurred to him. He spoke cautiously to Andreno, "Know thá th' anger thá story be causin'?"

Andreno nodded solemnly.

Bandun looked uncomfortable then he continued, "Be remembr'd thá be th' on'y fair Irelman in Falmora?"

Andreno was stunned. It had never occurred to him that he might cause suspicion about his loyalties by his coloring. The possible danger to himself, once the story was told to Falmora, became obvious.

Andreno's face grew even paler, but he looked directly at Bandun.

"Aye," he said quietly. "Un be remembr'd."

Bandun reached out and clasped Andreno's forearm.

"Th' council be called?" he asked.

"Aye, call th' council," answered Andreno. He lay back on the pallet, exhausted. Without another word Bandun jumped to his feet and hurried out to gather the men.

By the time the sun had fully lit the glade all people of Falmora were gathered in a tight circle around the largest fire. With their layered winter furs, they seemed like a clutch of oddly-shaped animals gathered for defense and warmth. There was a low excited murmur among them, for they knew that Fendun was to be forgiven, but they also sensed something more in Bandun's call to them for council.

Andreno had to be helped, partially carried, to the meeting. He was wrapped in winter skins and extra sleeping skins, and a pallet was laid for him close to the fire. As soon as he was sitting, the group exhaled a satisfied "Ahh" and all sat around him.

"Un be come to speak forgiveness o' Dun," Andreno began.

All around, the people nodded.

"Th' tellin' o' it brings need for decision o' all. Thá must say what should be done."

A murmur ran through the group and each looked at the others for some clue to this pronouncement. Why would they need to make decisions in the matter, when Andreno was the only one who could speak forgiveness for Fendun's mistake?

The answer of course lay in the reason for Fendun's outburst: the exhumed carcass, and all the other investigations that Andreno had pursued. When he'd told his story through, Andreno felt the tension in the silence around him.

The first question was nonverbal: a woman near him looked at his face skeptically and with concern. Andreno shook his head sadly, "No. Un be not fever'd still," he answered her.

Unwilling to accept a story of murder and willful lies among Irelmen, the people of Falmora offered comments on possible explanations for what Andreno had discovered.

"Be it that Havar be not full-witted?" offered one.

Another began: "Havar be forc'd in th' face o' enemies!"

"Be it th' Great One commanded..." came a half-finished suggestion.

"No!" screamed Andreno. His pent-up anger burst out on this sea of offered excuses. He pushed himself unsteadily to his feet.

"Havar spoke lies with full knowin'. Havar plotted to break Irelmen apart, to keep separate holdin', to keep secrets o' weaponry, to keep thá brothers from th' glade.

"Havar tells thá not to eat th' squirrel—keepin' Falmora weak an' hungry, an' providin' a cache o' meat for th' traitors.

"Havar tells thá to cast out th' old ones—keepin' thá stories from bein' told, an' keepin' Falmora away from truth.

"Havar tells thá o' all thá kinsmen slain by fierce fightin'—keepin' Falmora from knowin' th' fair-haired kinsmen be alive in a great Northr'n place..."

Andreno lost strength and crumpled back to the ground, sweating. The people shifted their bodies, uneasy. Each was thinking over all that had been told and trying to grasp the sadness and fury of it. One man looked to Andreno and Bandun.

"Be this full truth?" he asked them.

Andreno gave a tired nod, and Bandun answered, "Aye."

Another man jumped to his feet. "Why be it? For what reason did Havar cause a breakin' o' kinsmen? Be it that a break be needed, why not call a council? Why a slaughter an' lies?"

Bandun looked nervously at Andreno and started to stand to explain, but Andreno grabbed his arm and stopped him. Andreno spoke without rising. In shame he said, "Havar holds fair-haired Irelmen above all others, believin' thé be stronger, braver, havin' more wits, an' all ways better than th' dark kinsmen o' Falmora. Havar holds a diffr'nce o' color to be a diffr'nce o' men, believin' th' fair Irelmen bein' closer to th' Great One."

Some of the women began to cry softly and all the people looked stricken. Then some of the faces turned toward Andreno with anger. Bandun was ready for this moment. He sprang to his feet and spoke quickly, "'Tis much to be knowin' at one time. Thá think on this. On th' morrow un go to seek out Dun. On returnin' th' council be called again."

There were small grumblings, but the people considered the proposal fair. Gradually each moved to begin the day's work or gather in small groups to talk. Some approached Andreno to lay a hand on his shoulder in quiet support before leaving the gathering; but, many more left without a word and cast suspicious looks back over their shoulders,

As Bandun helped Andreno back to the tree, he thought over the hatred and resentment that had been unleashed among the people of Falmora. He too felt a great rage within his chest at the injustice and trickery that had enveloped their lives. He felt a great need to slash out and right the wrongs. But in his heart he knew the danger of this anger. What path would revenge forge? For the sake of the sons of Falmora, Bandun yearned for a wise solution.

CHAPTER 9
WARY ALLIANCE

When Lónae returned to the cave, the winter evening light was fading quickly. Fendun had built up the fire more than was necessary and bright firelight lit up his camp and reached halfway into the cave. By the light of the fire, they stored Lónae's provisions at the back of the cave and arranged her sleeping skins in the only available space—next to Dun's. As Lónae stored away her extra flying spears, she felt Dun watching her and spoke to break the unease.

"Thá would know this weapon?" She held up her sheaf of small spears.

Dun nodded vigorously,

"On th' morrow thá will know it," she offered.

Dun nodded in agreement and could think of nothing more to say. For a moment they stood awkwardly looking around their small cave. Then Fendun asked, "Be thá hungry?"

"Aye," Lónae smiled.

They cooked mashed roots and berries and drank gourds of hot tea. Lónae pulled two strips of dried meat from one of her pouches and offered one to Fendun. He recoiled instinctively at the taboo, but he watched fascinated as Lónae ate. After watching her tear and chew several bites of the rich-colored brown meat, Dun's mouth watered.

Lónae stopped eating and glared at Dun.

"Th' eatin' o' squirrel be not more than is done by Havar an' thá kinsmen! Nor, is't an evil—but on'y in Falmora Glade. Thá be not in Falmora. Be thá own man an' choose. But thá will not put thá choice on un!"

Dun masked his surprise with anger and jumped up. He stomped out of the range of firelight and paced in a great arc around the edge of the camp. He thought that Lónae's judgement was too harsh—she had never lived under the taboo, but he would someday return to the glade and the teachings of Havar. Fendun stood still. The winter chill seemed to shake through his body and pass into his soul. All this day, he had pondered Lónae's story and had finally come to accept the truth of it; but until this moment he had not consciously realized that acceptance meant that the rules of Havar held no meaning.

Fendun was suddenly an exile, not only because of his circumstance, but more fully now because of his new knowledge. If he did return to Falmora, it would no longer be a place of refuge, but a place of false habits. How could he explain the truth to the people when they already believed they lived it?

Then another realization came to him. Andreno must have known part of this new truth—that would explain Reno's actions in the forest; and also it explained why Reno's forgiveness was so long in coming: there was more at stake than Fendun's exile.

What action is right when the rules are no longer clear? Fendun stopped walking and squatted on his haunches. The dark forest seemed to be listening, patiently waiting for his decision. In the glade, decisions would be settled by discussion from all the people, but how would he come to new decisions alone? Fendun's eyes settled on the campfire in the distance. Lónae's words came back to him: *Be thá own man.* He shivered in the cold, rose up and slowly walked back to the fire.

As he entered the ring of firelight, Lónae half rose to her feet and started to speak, but Fendun held up his hand to silence her. He squatted by the fire near her and she sat back down.

Fendun turned full face toward Lónae. His great need to talk about his thoughts was clear in his anxious face.

"Be this true? A man knows what be right first by word o' th' Great One, but next, by word o' th' people an' what be best for all?"

"Aye," answered Lónae, "tis true."

Fendun took a deep breath and continued, "Be th' people find th' rules false, thé say anew what must be done. An' when a lone man find th' rules be false an' thar be no people to call in council—who will say what be right?" Fendun searched Lónae's eyes, asking the question for himself and at the same time seeking an answer from someone who had never known a community of men.

Lónae had never considered this dilemma, but her answer was unhesitating. She raised her hand in a fist and patted her chest softly. "Thá knowin' be here in all ways. Be thá with creatures in th' forest, thá follow in th' forest rules—kill when in need an' no more, in all times other, let pass by. Be thá with men—tis not diffr'nt."

"Thá canno' kill a man as a creature!" protested Fendun.

Lónae shook her head, "No. Not as a creature—on'y in need."

Fendun thought for a moment and then said, "Aye. May be tis true, be a man on'y alone. But men seek others for help in danger an' injury, to speak o' many thoughts, an' to laugh. An' men seek comfort o' brothers an' companions. With many men together, a lone man's knowin' be not enough for what be right."

Lónae shook her head again. "Each man has knowin' o' what be right—an' thé let all others pass by on th' path."

The great difference in the lives they had led came clearer to Fendun. He saw the circular pattern their talk was weaving. He was suddenly very tired and wanted only to sleep, but he'd regained some confidence through their discussion and he changed the focus of his musings.

"Thá be lone in th' forest an' thá seek another." He pointed to himself. "An' un be glad o' that," he added quickly. "But—in one day on'y, with gatherin' o' two Irelmen, thar be not full knowin' o' what be right, with all to say in agreein'."

Lónae opened her mouth to speak and then slowly closed it. She looked at the fire, thinking of the inadequacy of her answer in the face of Fendun's obvious anguish. She realized he was right—at least about the yearning of people—she had sought his company. She was no longer alone with her own rules. She looked at Fendun.

"Aye," she said softly, "Thar be more to men than th' rules o' forest creatures."

Though still not in full understanding, they had come to a temporary peace. In unspoken agreement, they prepared the fire for the night and gathered in their weapons and drinking gourds.

As they prepared for sleep, each was suddenly shy in the other's presence. In silence they removed their outer furs and spread them as extra coverings over their sleeping furs. Fendun pulled the skin covering over the mouth of the cave and only the faintest firelight shown in around the edges. Wrapped in their separate furs they felt glad not to be facing the winter alone. Lónae whispered into the dark, "May th' night embrace thá an' keep thá from harm."

"Aye," answered Fendun, "May th' night bring on'y peace..."

Fendun jumped as Lónae reached out to touch him. Then he relaxed for the first time since his exile and fell immediately to sleep.

The next morning the wind was blowing and the sky was overcast in dull brown-gray clouds. The scent of moisture hung in the air. Fendun and Lónae quickly ate and then made preparations for the coming storm. They moved firewood into the cave and stacked it across the back, in front of the food stores. Then they prepared a stone containment for the fire, just inside the cave mouth, to one side. By stacking stones in a circle and building up one side as a smoke deflector, they could safely light the fire inside the cave and, by opening the skin covering at the mouth just a little, draw the smoke outside.

After their work was done, Lónae showed Fendun how to string the bow and nock the flying spears. They took turns shooting at a small tree trunk. By the time the daylight had faded, Fendun had mastered the new weapon. The swiftness and reach of the small spears pleased him. Even in the wind, the flying spears were more accurate than any spear thrown by hand.

In the cave, they cooked mashed roots, nuts and berries. Sometimes the twisting winds would push toward the cave mouth and force a gust of smoke back into the cave, but most of the time the smoke was drawn out through the small crack of the mouth left uncovered. In the warmth and flickering light, neither Allialónae nor Fendun was tempted to break the tentative peace with more discussion of how to determine what is right. Instead, they turned to practical things. Lónae taught Fendun how to attach the small bird feathers to the notched ends of the flying spears. Fendun gathered all empty gourds and set them close to the mouth of the cave. He volunteered to keep vigil that night and scoop snow away from the cave mouth if it started to pile up.

As Lónae settled under her sleeping furs, Fendun crouched by the fire and slowly reviewed all the new information he'd gained in the last few days. There were many parts which he could not resolve, and many things which he did not understand: such as the motives for Havar's actions. Eventually, as the night progressed and the winds howled, his thoughts came back to his possible return to Falmora. He wondered what Andreno's thoughts were. How would Andreno determine what is right? Could it be that the forgiveness of Fendun did not fit into Andreno's decisions? The possibility of permanent exile so disturbed Fendun that he had no difficulty staying awake.

CHAPTER 10
DELAY

Overnight, Falmora Glade silently filled with snow. Protected on all sides by forest, the glade formed no wind-driven snow drifts, but the wind howled across the tops of the trees and dipped madly down into the opening of the glade, leaving great rounded depressions in the snow.

Most of the Irelmen were awakened in the night by the howling wind, but they soon returned to sleep. Andreno could not sleep. The decision to bring back Fendun would have been enough to give him peaceful sleep; however, when he heard the winds and looked out to see the massive fall of snow, Andreno's heart fell. He spent the night in frustrated anger at being blocked from the one action that could ease his guilt. He pushed away all thoughts of Fendun's safety: he would not allow himself to imagine possibilities of injury or exposure.

At daylight, snow was still falling, though not as heavy as the night fall. By unspoken agreement, Andreno and Bandun were awake before dawn and met solemn-faced at Bandun's table. Bandun could barely contain his frustration and he paced, fidgeted and made tea in disappointed silence until, finally, trusting himself to speak, he stated the obvious. "Th' storm brings delay."

Andreno had no ready answer to Bandun's worry; for he felt it too. However, he could not accept the delay as a defeat and he soon offered encouragement. "Thá taught Dun well in all things—to hunt, to seek shelter, to preserve 'is life," Andreno began. Bandun sat straighter and puffed his chest in pride at the praise.

Andreno continued, "Dun be waitin' as we be ready to go—but 'e will not have left aside th' lessons 'e larn'd from Dun th' Elder. Dun bides safe until we come for 'im!" Andreno spoke with total conviction, as if he knew that Fendun's safety was assured. He needed desperately to believe it and would not allow doubts to form. Bandun grasped at the show of confidence and braced his own hopes. With no alternative he sealed their thoughts about what should be done.

"Aye," said Bandun. "Thar be no wisdom in a search through such as this. At first sign o' spring an' snowmelt—we bring Dun forgiveness an' lead 'im to Falmora."

The harsh winter grip sealed all Irelmen from venturing from their protected refuges. This time of enforced enclosure was well spent. Household goods were mended or shaped anew. Squirrel skins were patched and sewn for clothing and bedding. Tunnels were dug through the deep snow between caves and tree bases until all the households connected in an eerie network of silent icy hallways. Around the evening fires, ancient tales were repeated and the adventures of the recent summers were recounted, often with the actions acted out by the teller for the delight of the listeners.

At first, each Irelman kept the new knowledge of Andreno's confessions in silent consideration. Then as the winter advanced and their close company grew more relaxed, they began to discuss the treachery of Havar openly. Everyone agreed on the despicable nature of the treason, but no two Irelmen could come to terms about what action should be taken. More than once, the discussion escalated to shouts which echoed hollowly across the silent snow-packed glade. And one evening the arguments became so heated that a wrestling match, engaged to break the tension, caused two Irelmen to tear through the skin covering on an upper tree entrance and plummet madly into the crisp snow below. Luckily, the snowfall had accumulated to such a depth that the men were not hurt by their fall, and in the freezing darkness the muffled sounds of continued combat wafted up from the hole created in the snow. Amid cheers and backslaps the Irelmen made wagers on which of the two fallers may have landed on his back and thus lost the match. However, it took many hands and much labor to tunnel through to the two wrestlers and lead them back to the warmth of the fires. By the time they were rescued, the wrestlers had given up trying to convince each other by force, but the point of the argument was not given up and the contention smoldered.

In the Northern camp of Havar, a false calm prevailed. The blond Irelmen completed the same winter chores as their dark kinsmen, but in the story-telling hours there was an undercurrent of unease. The people gathered in companionship around evening fires, but few reclined in relaxed good humor—most sat alert or stood, and each kept a bundle of flying spears slung across his back or close beside him.

Many things about Innismoor were strange to Fanáh. The absence of the protective towering forest was enough to cause her anguish, for the vast emptiness of the moors seemed to manifest her feelings of loneliness. But the way the people were forced to live in this new place was unsettling. There were a few shallow caves, but no great amount of trees, so the people lived in stone cave structures which they built themselves. They covered the tops with a woven frame of small limbs and layered the frames with bog grasses and peat. In place of firewood they burned dried chunks of peat which continually smoked and filled each stone cavern with a foggy haze.

Although warmed by the winter fires, Fanáh did not find the open companionship she yearned for. Her arrival at Innismoor seemed to create no suspicion. Her years of isolation in the forest made her eccentric enough that her story of disorientation was believable. However, none drew close to her, and her separation from Allialónae gave her more sorrow than she had expected.

Ignored in her loneliness, considered odd but harmless, Fanáh roamed freely to various gatherings and listened at the edge of the winter talks. What she heard made her uneasy. The stories did not center on elaborate rememberings and imagined possibilities, nor even on the ancient tales. Instead, the people talked of methods of defense and tactics of battle. All stories centered on the superior triumphs of the warriors of Innismoor. And in hushed tones, the mention of Havar and his laws ran through all talk. Fanáh was disturbed by the free speaking of Havar's full name, for she was convinced that Havar still lived; and although Havar's people broke all the rules set down for the people of Falmora, no one should ever intentionally break the rules of the Great One. Each time someone pronounced Havar's full name, Fanáh shivered and inadvertently cast her eyes toward the stone-cave hut which was isolated from all the others.

Very few people ever approached the solitary cave-hut, and only a few of the warriors were ever seen to enter there. The perimeter of the hut was always guarded by sentries. Within the dank and gloomy stone enclosure, Havar crouched. His twisted bent form swayed close to the small fire and his crooked hands slowly opened and closed in the air above the smoldering peat as he tried to grab the heat before it rose. His long grey hair, thinned and yellowed by campfires and time, tendrilled out on all sides of his large head and seemed a part of the smoky haze. Bulging veins on his wide forehead throbbed with the slow rhythm of his long life and traced a blue-black pattern under his skin, down through his weak and wrinkled neck and back into the dark cavern of his chest where his evil soul's heart pulsed it back again.

Intermittent low groaning growls escaped through his slack parched lips in unconscious protest of the aches that throbbed through his aged body. But despite his discomfort, when his thoughts touched on particular favored memories, his lips worked together in savory smacking sounds and then stretched back in a tight and mirthless grin. His dark eyes shone with undepleted energy as Havar gloated on his power.

As she felt the tenseness surrounding her, Fanáh's thoughts went back to Angara and his ravings against Havar. Angara's warnings gained validity for Fanáh. After their years together yearning in separate directions, Angara's words finally settled as truth in Fanáh's mind. At first she sighed at the injustice of discovering a true path too late, then she remembered the possible arrival of Allialónae in Innismoor and she determined to be prepared for whatever action was required to save them both.

Fanáh began to slip away from the encampment unobserved. On the windy moors, hidden by the heather and small trees in the shallow valleys, she honed new flying spears and practiced shooting until her aim was perfect. Around in several caches amidst the peat and rocks, Fanáh hid bundles of spears. She would practice and watch and when the time came, she would escape with Lónae and together they would return to Falmora.

Although no one from the encampment took notice of Fanáh, there was one who watched from the distant high moors. Angara was glad at the sight of Fanáh training alone with her flying spears—for he knew immediately that she had matched her thoughts to his at last. The knowledge of her allegiance gave him the only sense of comfort he had known since they parted.

The last three years had been a harsh lonely trial for Angara. He had lived and slept without shelter, constantly moving his camp— watching the people of Havar. He will never give up his need for revenge. If he watches long enough, he knows a weak thread will show in the cloth that binds Havar's tribe. Fanáh's secret actions may be the clue to the first unravelling.

From where he crouched in the heather, Angara's body leaned forward in yearning toward the distant sight of Fanáh. He longed to go to her and touch her and show her he was real—his full name had not yet been called by the Great One. But he knew he must wait for the right time—he would know when it was time. Allialónae's absence bothered him. Was she pledged to the cause of Havar? Did she move in the inner encampment? He watched the campfires for sight of her familiar form, but never saw her in the circles of people. Perhaps the forest had overcome her; perhaps she had not come North with Fanáh, and she wandered alone in the winter. Angara stopped his thoughts. Allialónae must be safe, wherever she was—for he had taught her well and she knew the ways of the wild.

CHAPTER II
WATCHER IN THE FOREST

Through the waves of winter storms, Fendun and Allialónae worked together to survive. Each traded nights to be sentinel when it was necessary to guard the cave opening against the danger of piled snow. However, most evenings they worked together in the shelter of the cave and told stories of their childhood. Fendun listened in rapt attention to Lónae's stories. She grew up amidst the forest creatures and knew their habits better than the best hunter from Falmora. She, in turn, was fascinated by Fendun's tales of community and the actions of the people as they lived in a group. Lónae was especially interested in the tales of the birth celebrations. She leaned her chin in her hand and smiled, wide-eyed as Fendun described the games, contests and foods.

"It were a birth ceremony when last un be in Falmora Glade," Fendun explained one evening, then he stood, as was custom, to pronounce the baby's full name, "Tunendan," and that of its parents, "son o' Jardán an' Myraynah." Then Fendun sat and told of the small baby and the people's joy, and of his own birth.

"In th' time o' Reno's birth, un were born one day afore. It were as a twin birth—an' Reno as un brother. A full week o' celebrate!" Fendun sat up tall with the words and his eyes shone with pleasure. Then he slumped in gloom and was silent.

Allialónae considered him for a moment, then she asked softly, "Tell un of thá brother, Reno."

Fendun hung his head and slowly shook it. Lónae reached to him and laid her hand on his. He looked up. Lónae nodded encouragement,

"Reno be th' cause of thá banishment, though not th' full reason for it. Tell what's in thá heart an' leave th' unknown for Reno's tellin'."

Fendun stared at the fire and began, "Reno be good in all things, 'e knows th' way o' th' hunt an' th' killin' o'squirrel—most, 'e knows to make things to please th' eye. Reno be clever in carvin' an' craftin' o' wares." Fendun sat up straight and pointed to his chest, "'E be like Dun in manners all—though unlike as to look on. Reno be more in height an' less wide—though still strong. An 'e be fair."

Lónae's eyebrows rose. "Fair? Fair, an' be in Falmora?"

"Aye," answered Fendun, glum again.

But Lónae would not let him lag. "Reno walks as one among th' people? No one marks 'im fair?"

Fendun nodded, then shook his head, then sat perplexed as Lónae jumped to her feet. "A fair Irelman not o' Havar! O' th' people o' Falmora an' brother-friend to Dun! Un will go to Reno—un will be with Falmora!"

Fendun drew back a little from the fire. He considered Allialónae in silence. In part he knew why she was excited—to think of entering the glade of Falmora, to be in the company of the Irelmen and not to be the only one of fair hair. But there seemed more to her excitement, something more in her eagerness to seek out Reno. And he felt a twinge of envy as he compared the mental vision of his strongly built, but shorter dark image to that of Reno's lithe, but still manly, fair and taller form. What would Lónae make of the comparison when at last she saw them together? Would she be drawn to one more like herself? And so, what if she were attracted to Reno?

Fendun looked silently at Allialónae with the question still in his eyes. Lónae sat opposite him and had also fallen silent—although her eyes were still alive with her anticipation. As she met Fendun's gaze, she smiled—and Fendun knew that what she thought mattered to him very much. His comparison with Reno was unavoidable—but Lónae must prefer the company of Fendun, for in his heart he had already chosen her.

As the days imperceptibly grew longer, Allialónae and Fendun knew each other well by the recitation of their life experiences. They also knew where their differences ran to argument and although they did not consciously avoid disagreements—for points of contention often provided good entertainment on drab winter evenings—their conversation never returned to the matter of how to decide what is truly right. By avoiding direct discussion of rules and living only by unspoken guidelines, they were often led in their actions by instinct more than habit.

One day, in the earliest part of spring, when the cold still held and the trees and plants remained dormant gray, the scent of the air changed from dry to moist and carried the first insistent suggestion of warmth. The bird songs changed from the cautious abrupt twitters of winter to raucous testing notes that would soon carry into full song when the leaves returned to camouflage.

Fendun and Lónae were drawn from their cave. Though the air was cold, the sun was bright and they were restless to have release from their winter confinement. They packed provisions for the day in squirrel skin pouches and walked into the forest to explore. Fendun carried his own pouch of flying spears slung across his shoulder, but had no curving stick to fling them. He would search the forest for one of correct size that could be bent and strung. Lónae showed him the best type of wood but cautioned that they should not cut the length until the weather warmed and the wood began to awaken from winter sleep and became more pliant.

By midday they were in deep forest and sought out a spring to drink from as they ate. Lónae led and they came to a very quiet copse where the twigs of the leafless undergrowth were so thick they gave shelter even in winter. Around the spring source, water trickled over smooth rocks for a few feet then disappeared underground again. Over all, the branches and brambles formed a natural canopy,

Pleased by the bird sounds, softened now through the many layers of overgrowth, Fendun and Lónae sat by the stream and in unspoken agreement kept silent. Slowly they ate dried berries and nuts and scooped handfuls of cold water from the spring. In the shelter of the copse the wind could not penetrate and the still air was welcoming. Warmed by their walking and relaxed from eating, the two, now by habit, spread out their outer furs side by side on the soft moss and leaves and lay down. Fendun lay on his back and stared intently up through all the tangled vines and branches, searching for sight of the sky. Silently, Lónae laid her face close to his—looking up too—trying to see what it was he searched for. Immediately, a rising strength formed between them, like a warm wind ruffling within their bodies at the same time. They felt a longing force outside their intent, but emanating from within. Without pause or question they silently shed all coverings and drew close in total trust. The shocking velvet touch of skin against skin overwhelmed all thoughts and cares. They moved instinctually together in ancient rhythm with all life surrounding them.

In the powerful union of their bodies, Fendun and Lónae felt the merging of their beings—a strength of two as one. Lulled by this new security, they were unaware of the shifting winds above them gathering clouds. Suddenly, even in their close warmth, their skin chilled with the abrupt wave of coming cold. Lónae sat up quickly and moved to the spring. Fendun watched fascinated as she splashed the clear water over her smooth skin. Her body glistened; very slender, but strong in her arms and legs—and wonderfully different from Fendun's in the surprising female roundness of her hips and breasts.

His staring trance was broken as he realized how dark the forest was. Moving quickly, he bathed water on his own body and dressed, still damp. Lónae rubbed dry with a clump of dried grass and was fully dressed as Fendun gathered their weapons. As they rushed from their sheltered grotto the stinging force of the coming storm hit them. The moist smell of spring had reverted to winter and flakes of snow were already swirling madly in the wind. Chased by the certain doom of being caught in the storm, they fled without caution toward the shelter of their cave. This time Fendun led.

For a while the snow fell so thick and fast that Fendun reached his hand back to grasp Allialónae's as they crashed through the underbrush. They took no care to be cautious about making noise, for it was more important to reach the cave quickly before the storm totally blinded their way than to move stealthily to avoid alerting squirrels.

As they pushed forward, Fendun held his forearm above his eyes as a shield against the stinging snow. With his other arm extended back to lead Lónae, he was not prepared to grab for his weapons when the dark form appeared before them, hazy through the snow. The figure made no move to greet or attack, but somehow seemed unsurprised as if he had been waiting. In his surprise, Fendun stopped without warning and Lónae, still lunging forward, collided into his back. The impact sent both off balance and they fell. Even as they went down, Fendun kept his eyes on the blurry shape and saw the man hurry sideways out of their path and disappear in the snow and trees.

Fendun helped Lónae to stand and looked quickly all around them. It was impossible to see anything in the falling maze of snow.

"What be thar?" Lónae asked. Making a quick decision, Fendun said only, "It be naught," grabbed her hand again and began to run. He pulled more insistently, urging Lónae to hurry. Perhaps they would elude the strange watcher in the storm and make it to the cave undetected.

Before they had run far, both saw the form faintly running parallel to them—but when they stopped, the man stopped too and instead of approaching them, he pivoted and retreated.

For a moment they stood and tried to peer through the whiteness, but saw no movement. Without speaking, they hurried on, glancing to each side as they went.

By midafternoon they had reached the cave and were confined there for two days until the weather again softened and the snow began to melt slowly. Though they could once again range far from the cave, they kept a self-imposed limit on their wandering, for the unknown man was somehow forbidding. Why did he appear to be only watching them? Was he watching them still?

Though the watcher in the forest gave them caution in their actions, Lónae and Fendun were well satisfied to keep close to the cave and to each other.

CHAPTER 12
DISQUIET AND PREPARATION

Disquieted by their changed knowledge of Havar, the Irelmen of Falmora Glade were at odds with each other. Some thought that Andreno's words were in some way a trick, meant to confuse them and disrupt their harmony. Others thought Andreno's information was revealed in good intention and would serve to unite them in strong cause. Whatever thoughts swayed their opinion about Andreno, each Irelman instinctively knew that the course of their lives would not continue as it had. If Havar was not planning to infiltrate their glade, then they would surely seek out Havar. In either event they would be prepared as warriors first, and kinsmen second, for Havar's actions had given them no doubt that he held low regard for kinship—if he considered it at all.

Not since the time of the ancients had the Irelmen of Falmora prepared for battle. Now in the quiet of winter, their extra time was turned to forging of weapons and all supplies of war. When unobserved, the Irelwomen wept at the cause for this new activity; and in their hearts, the Irelmen wept too, for they sensed what misery their actions would bring and they wished for it to be over before it had even begun.

For Andreno, the preparations for battle gave a respite from the torture of waiting for spring and his journey to find Fendun. Although he limped badly from his wound, Andreno was able to walk and he moved slowly but insistently from one group of Irelmen to the next, overseeing the preparations. A few resented his directions but most welcomed the knowledge he offered. Everyone respected Andreno's skill as a craftsman and when his ability was coupled with his new knowledge of the weapons being used by Havar, Reno's word was usually well accepted.

Each worked to make a shield of squirrel skin stretched taut over wood and bone frames. Slings were made or repaired for stones and extra pouches and provisions were set aside. Since none had ever made the flying spears or bow, the task became a full group endeavor. Andreno had found several flying spears and it was not long after concentrated efforts that most Irelmen were able to duplicate the size and heft of the slender spears. The task that remained unmastered was the perfection of a curved bow. After much trial and error the frame of the bow itself was achieved—in as many different designs as there were Irelmen, for each bow was unique in its particular curve and inlay of bone and wood, and each was carved with a design or figure somewhere along its length. The part that was a mystery was the strengthening of the bowstring. Many methods were tried but all resulted in a short-lived string. Eventually, the best method agreed upon was to braid very fine strips of tanned squirrel skin and coat the strands with bee's wax.

Even with setbacks, the Irelmen were preparing well in supplies and arms. Yet no one was attending to the methods of conflict and to what leader all would accept and follow. The Irelmen of Bandun's age—though willing to fight and able enough—were reluctant to push forward. The younger men of Andreno's age felt their lack of experience all too clearly, and though filled with strength, they lacked complete conviction in their purpose.

More by lack of opposition than by open support, Andreno became the leading force of the Irelmen of Falmora. His young energy and burning sense of the injustices done to Falmora served well to fuel his drive for revenge and inspired his kinsmen. The spark of his deep anger was essential to urge the others to action, but his practical knowledge lay only in new ideas and craftsmanship. Help in the knowledge Reno lacked came from two unlikely sources.

Throughout his days and evenings of surveying the progress of weapons, Andreno had a constant companion. His father, Farliam, who had ignored Andreno and all others for many years, gave total interest to the new activities. After so much time inattentive to others, Farliam had been accepted as simple. Now, he followed Andreno's every step and showed keen interest and a strong new awareness in his gaze. Liam still spoke to no one, but he was agile and very patient, and as Reno guided the Irelmen's hands to perfect their weapons, Liam began to follow directly after and silently demonstrate skill in using the weapons. Without a word he would gently lay his hands on the practicing warriors—turning one man sideways who was too forward-facing to shoot the flying spears accurately; correcting another's stance to give better leverage as he hurled a spear; showing many the skills of patient preparation, concealment, and true marksmanship. When an Irelman would face Liam to thank him for instruction, they received an unsettling direct gaze, piercing in sadness—and they had to turn their eyes away. Still, they recognized his great skill and many were the welcome greetings "Aruh, Liam," as he approached their fires.

In their separate ways, each Irelman grew competent individually to handle the new weapons as well as the old. As a group, they had no sense of oneness. Jardán, father of the infant Tunendan, observed the dispersion of the Irelmen's separate strengths and knew the need to bring them together. Though he was several years older than Andreno, Jardán approached him as an equal. One morning before Andreno had finished his gourd of tea, Jardán approached his fire.

Reno looked up, expectant, "Aruh, Dan." he welcomed.

Jardán nodded. Abruptly he began, "Do thá see th' weakness left in this?"

Reno looked surprised, for through all the preparations no one had been willing to actually speak about their actions. Now he answered with a sense of relief at Jardán's directness, "Aye, thé be many not yet full-practiced."

Jardán nodded impatiently and said, "'Tis not a great weakness— it will be larn'd."

He suddenly squatted close to Andreno and lowered his voice in insistent council: "What plan be thar to carry the whole as one? When to press on an' when to go back? Whar to stand or lie, an' in what groups? Who will pass th' word o' what to do—an' how will it be known whose word is first to follow?" Jardán realized he had been leaning ever closer to Reno with each question. He jumped to his feet and stepped back in apology. Then he spoke again, his voice rising, "Thar be no plan for th' whole—thar needs a decidin' afore Falmora be cast out at Havar!"

Reno struggled to his feet and forced his wounded leg into painful steps. He placed a hand on Jardán's shoulder and looked gratefully into the face of this unexpected ally.

"Thá speak true, Dan. Tell un thá plan."

Jardán's face relaxed and he took a breath that swelled his chest. Slowly he breathed out in relief — though never enough to smile. His dark blue eyes stared into Reno's pale ones and found an instant understanding. Formally, he answered, "Come thá, Reno, to un tree, as th' sun reaches th' mid-glade." Then he turned without waiting for an answer and walked away to his tree. Reno watched after him with mixed feelings of gratitude and an unnamed fear.

At mid-day, Reno climbed to Jardán's tree. At the highest entryway they were able to look out over all the glade and observe each group of Irelmen below. Jardán explained that from this vantage point one of them could direct group movements to practice tactics while the other organized from the ground. They could plan events between them and each day give surprise practice plans to the Irelmen.

Reno agreed immediately; and it was obvious that Jardán should direct from above while Reno led from the ground level. With Liam and Dan to help in the areas where Reno was weak, the practices became more intense and purposeful, but at the same time it gave Reno more freedom to contemplate what was most urgent to him—the coming of spring and Fendun's forgiveness.

Tanéha, along with the other Irelwomen, worked on the periphery of the war preparations. They too helped to gather extra provisions, tan squirrel skins and make extra foot coverings and food pouches. But in the evenings, their talk avoided the subject that all their efforts strived toward.

They talked of herbs and the coming spring and the antics of the Irel babies—and many things except the coming conflict which would take all the Irelmen from the glade. Tanéha was very quiet among the Irelwomen. She could think of nothing else but Reno's leaving, and talking of other things did not dispel the heavy dread within her. During his recovery, she had stayed by his side day and night; but since he had moved out of Bandun's tree, he lived alone again and she had returned to her parents. Reno had been more like himself since declaring his intention to forgive Fendun and he once again talked freely with Tanéha; but the preparations for battle kept him more often away from her and she longed to be at his side again.

One evening Tanéha walked with Andreno as he completed a circumference of the glade, thinking over the day's work, planning for tomorrow—foremost, planning his search for Fendun.

The night air was cold and Reno's injury made his gait stiff.

"Be thá pained?" asked Néha, glancing at Reno's leg.

"No," Reno answered, "Ne'er much pain—on'y slow an' hard in movin'."

Tanéha latched her arm in Reno's. "Soon thá seek Dun?"

"Aye, an' will not wait for warmth—in spring all Irelmen take revenge o' Havar!"

"Un go with thá to seek Dun!" Tanéha declared.

Andreno stopped and faced Tanéha. She looked at him earnestly.

Reno spoke softly, "We be not mated, Néha. Thá canno' travel day an' night alone so with un."

"Be us mated on th' morrow—un an' thá," Néha answered.

Reno instantly glared at this mention of mating day which was solely his right to suggest. Then Néha's complete anguish flashed in response to his anger and she turned her back and hid her face in her hands. Reno felt an ache in his chest and he reached out to touch Néha's back.

"Thar be not time, Néha. Un leave to seek Dun in three days, or four—or two. We be mated in fall when all th' battle be over an' Dun be here for th' celebrate."

Tanéha whirled and hugged him fiercely. Against his chest she spoke, "An' be thá slain in battle, or be thá lost in search o' Dun? We be not mated—ever." Tanéha looked into Reno's face and knew his thoughts. "Thar be no need for celebrate, Reno. Thar be not time nor food. In fall, when thá be returned—an' Dun—thar be a celebrate for all things."

Reno clasped Néha to him softly in silence. He thought of all that must be done before they might again hold each other so. He thought of all the changes brought to Falmora by the treachery of Havar, and of his own part in revealing the knowledge. And within a few minutes of silence he threw off accepted custom and brought one more abrupt change into their patterned glade—he unconditionally accepted Néha's boldness and wisdom.

And just as quickly as he reasoned the truth of Néha's words—all reason left him and the urgent warm closeness of their bodies overwhelmed him. Leading Tanéha quietly into the forest, Andreno lay down with her on the dark mounded softness of fallen leaves. Ignoring the cold, they quickly pulled away their outer coverings; and as the heat of their nakedness joined them together in instinctive union, all else was forgotten. They were at last one—truly mated.

Finally, very gently, Reno said, "Aye, Néha, in all ways thá speak true. On th' morrow, un an' thá be mated, for we be not meant to stay as separate—even in four days, or two."

CHAPTER 13
EVIL WAITS

In the dark man-made cave which had become his only and constant habitat, Havar was well at ease. His dark soul clung to the dank and dim interior of his confinement. He was old, like a corpse already inhabiting a spacious tomb, but his mind was strong and bent as ever to the base purpose of his life's endeavor. Havar was master of the people of Innismoor, and through them he was master also of the lesser people of Falmora. In this power he considered himself akin to the Great One—yet his rule would even improve upon the plan of the Great One, for Havar would bring purity to the people. With the final destruction of the dark-haired ones, all Irelmen would become true kinsmen in their bloodlines and stand fair-haired only to serve the glory of Havar.

When he thought of the task of eliminating the Falmorans, Havar was not discouraged. For these dark-haired simple ones had been so easy to fool in the past! He sighed with contentment when he thought about the small effort it took for his warriors to exhume the squirrel carcasses and dry the meat for Innismoor. The Falmorans took all the risk of the kill and grew weak with lack of meat—and all by his edict! And he would often chuckle dryly to himself when he thought of the other men of his age wandering aimlessly in the West, listening for their names—also by his decree! A smile of cruel satisfaction crossed his face as he reveled in the thought that he was the only old one whose voice was heard and acknowledged.

He sighed and closed his eyes in pleasure at his power. Havar the Great—that was another change he'd wrought. The people called him

Havar, by his full name. Almost immediately, Havar began to shake and glance around nervously as the fear of breaking the Great One's rule overcame him. Then he shrugged off the feeling and scowled at his weakness, relieved that none had observed him.

But in his cleverness, Havar had been too satisfied with his success and placed too little import on his weaknesses. Not all of the people of Innismoor were convinced of Havar's omnipotence and many were still uneasy about the changes he dictated. For these people, any sign of weakness in Havar was secretly noted and remembered. A subtle undercurrent of resentment was forming even in the face of the great fear the people had of Havar. Not only were there a few who remembered the peaceful times in Falmora and longed for that life, but many people resented the abolishment of the council meetings for making decisions. There was also a point on which all the people of Innismoor were equally unsettled: in the early years, Havar had taken more than one mate. Havar justified his action by saying that a great leader needed assurance of at least one male heir—but the people were deeply insulted by this break from basic instinct and ancient custom. And so, as the hint of spring arrived, the people of Innismoor were outwardly united in purpose, but inwardly divided by dissension.

In the early morning after their decision, Andreno called a council meeting in the glade and he and Tanéha announced their intentions and their promise to each other. The people were very tired from the tension and physical preparations of battle, and at first they stood in silence after Andreno spoke. Then a quiet murmuring began among them and one of the men spoke out, "Thá tell of false rules set by Havar—an' now thá will change all else?"

"Aye!" an Irelwoman quickly added, "An' forgettin' th' celebrate, too?"

Then Bandun stood up and crossed his arms across his chest. He spoke low, with barely controlled anger, "Aye, an' one thing more be still undone!" He glared at Andreno for daring to forget Fendun.

Andreno raised his arms for silence. "Un be not wantin' to change, nor bring one diffr'nce more on Falmora. It be that un will lead all Irelmen to Innismoor—soon as spring be near—an' un be yearnin' to stay on'y in Falmora." Andreno's throat was suddenly tight and he looked down, fighting his fears and longings. Then quickly he looked up again at the faces waiting for him to continue. "More change un do not seek for Falmora, on'y th' same as all Irelmen, un seek good will of th' council for un mating, Reno an' Néha." Again, Reno paused and his eyes were shiny with tears, but he did not look down, "For time be short—in all ways."

Silently the Irelmen nodded and one spoke up, "Be thá mated, Reno an' Néha, an' live thá long an' well in Falmora."

A soft murmur of consent spread through the gathered council.

Tanéha rose to stand by Andreno and he clasped her to him. "On this day, un be well pleased. May all Falmora come to th' celebrate—in th' time when all life folds to sleep an' cold winds be near, an' all Irelmen be returned to Falmora with no cares nor great harm."

Bandun still stood, unmoved. Andreno walked to him and in a voice for all to hear he said, "On first light for th' comin' day, un be gone to seek Dun an' bring un brother again to Falmora."

Bandun's face relaxed in total joy and he put out a hand on Andreno's shoulder; then, in overwhelming relief, he clasped Reno to him, pounding his back with alternate hugs and congratulations. Gradually the people moved forward and placed their hands on Andreno and Tanéha in blessing.

CHAPTER 14
REUNION

In their small cave, a larger world had formed for Fendun and Allialónae. With the first bonding of their bodies came a linking of their souls and they were content to limit their excursions to the close perimeters of their camp and explore the mystery of their new-found intimacy.

Although they both shared great pleasure and wonder in this new strength which united them their silent thoughts were very different. Without the strictures of a society, Allialónae had grown to accept all things directly as either good or bad. She had no concept of preconceived plots or intentions to deceive or hurt; and she lived as all other forest creatures: accepting natural events in the course of their occurrence. For Lónae, physical attachment to Fendun was good, and seemed only one great progression in all the events of her life.

Fendun brooded over the correctness of their actions. Although he didn't deny their bond was good and right, he anguished over the knowledge of having broken the rites of tradition. Lónae and Fendun were mated without the blessing of the council of Falmora, and although none were there to judge them, Fendun felt the judgment within himself. He worried, for he began to believe that he would return to Falmora—with Allialónae—yet even if he returned with Andreno's forgiveness, how would the people react when he brought Lónae as his mate, without consulting them? And in what way would they look upon his chosen one: an eater of squirrel meat, a female hunter—a fair-haired one?

As it happened, Fendun did not have to anguish long over his uncertainties. He was forced to face unanswered questions quite sooner than he had expected. He had often imagined a scene of reunion with images of him and Andreno facing each other in the forest, exchanging greetings and explanations and forgiveness and returning to Falmora together. In reality, his reunion with Reno came unexpectedly abrupt and more complicated than his daydreams.

One early morning, Lónae and Fendun sat close to their fire waiting for their mash of berries, nuts and water to warm and simultaneously saw a movement at the edge of the clearing. Andreno appeared, silently standing just within the forest. He was dressed in layers of winter skins and even his head and hands were covered against the cold. But Fendun knew him immediately—and he knew exactly in that instant that he was forgiven. His heart beat wildly as he jumped to his feet. At the same time, Lónae lunged for her bow and had nocked a flying spear in defense. As she brought the bowstring to her cheek and pulled it taut, Fendun cried out in horror, "Hold!" Lónae jumped at his shout and slowly lowered her weapon. She looked at Fendun's panicked face and back again at the silent figure by the trees—and then she too knew this was not the watcher in the forest.

Fendun cautioned her with a lowered voice, "Stay thá still an' not afraid—for truly tis Reno come for forgivin'."

They waited for Andreno to make the first movement.

Yet he stood silent, watching, and Fendun realized his brother was unsure of welcome. Slowly Fendun raised one hand in greeting and Andreno walked forward immediately. His gait was labored and uneven, and Fendun, fearing Reno had been injured in his search, rushed forward to meet him.

As they came face to face, they stood for a moment staring into each other's eyes. Then in spontaneous unity, they hugged each other fiercely, savoring for a minute just their closeness, without the entanglement of words. Then, urgently, as if to make up for all the time passed, Andreno said, "Thá be forgiv'n, Dun. Come thá back to Falmora."

Fendun's whole body slumped in relief at the sound of the words he had longed for. His eyes filled with tears and all he could do was nod. The two brothers held onto each other in a grip like a silent promise never again to be parted. Then, remembering Andreno's difficulty in walking, Fendun pushed away and searched him with anxious eyes, "Be thá hurt?" he asked.

Andreno gave a crooked half-smile. "Un hurt be mended with thá return." Then he glanced down at his legs, "Un be torn by squirrel bite an' though long-healed, th' mend be twisted."

Fendun looked at Reno expectantly, waiting to hear the story. But Andreno glanced past Fendun toward the fire.

"Be thá not alone?" Reno asked.

Fendun turned toward Lónae as though he was also surprised at her presence, then he said, "Come," grasped Reno's arm and led him toward the fire. Lónae stood waiting, her stance still defensive, the bow still clutched in her hand. Her long hair hung loose in a white-silver flow in the bright morning sun. As they approached, each was caught off-guard in their separate impressions. Andreno saw a curiously delicate small man whose pretty face was incongruous with his warrior garb—and whose untied hair proved his carelessness. Fendun saw incongruity of another type. There was a look of near fear on Lónae's face—a look he seldom saw in her usual forward approach to all events.

Standing between the two he loved most, Fendun was unsure how to begin. As in all important events, such as mating ceremonies or introductions for people not present at the birth celebration, it was accepted to pronounce the full names of those involved. He reached for Lónae's hand and placed it with his on Andreno's forearm and pronounced her name, "Allialónae," for Andreno. Then he looked anxiously at Reno—for he dared not say Andreno's full name aloud after all that had happened. Andreno saw the look of anxiety on Fendun's face and spoke his own name, "Andreno."

From the manner of Fendun's introduction, Andreno knew that Allialónae was not some small man, but a woman, and someone of great importance to Fendun. Although he was confused and uncomfortable with her clothing and weapons, Andreno also saw the fear in Lónae's face, and he was drawn to this fair-haired one. Instinctively, he swept back his head covering with his free hand to reveal his own light hair, correctly secured in back—now coiled in a warrior's knot. Then he reached to cover their hands with his.

The effect on Lónae was immediate. Although she knew from Fendun's stories that Andreno was fair-haired, she had never seen a man with hair such as her own and her mother, Fanáh's. And as Andreno extended his hand to touch hers and Fendun's, Lónae's manner eased and she quietly said, "Reno," as correctly as if she'd said his name all her life.

Andreno looked quickly in question at Fendun and then realized that this strange woman knew of him through Fendun's telling. He looked back at Allialónae, "How be thá called?"

"Lónae," she answered. She stared for a brief second into the eyes of this stranger who was so like her—the stranger whose name she already knew. Andreno stared back—held by her eyes.

Though it lasted only an instant, the shared look seemed to have a force of meaning hidden from Fendun's understanding. He reacted as if to danger, and pulled their hands away.

In the awkwardness of the moment, Lónae spoke quickly, "Be thá hungry?"

Andreno did not answer at first, but looked uncomfortable and turned to glance back at the forest. Then, remembering his manners, he answered, "Aye," but added, "Un be not alone."

Fendun's eyebrows raised and Lónae leaned to peer around Andreno toward the forest. "Who be with thá?" Fendun asked.

Andreno lifted his chin slightly and said formally, "Néha comes as mate to Reno." Fendun's brows rose even more, but before he could speak, Andreno continued, "An' too, thá father, Dun."

Fendun could not contain his excitement. He grasped Andreno's arm and his eyes darted in all directions. "Whar be thé? Be near?" he exclaimed.

Andreno clasped Fendun's shoulder in reassurance. "Be not far, an' waitin' to know what word o' Dun!"

"Go un, to th' place! Show un th' way!" demanded Fendun.

"Aye," agreed Reno. "'Tis but a short walk an' return." Fendun turned to Allialónae, "Keep thá th' fire, Lónae, an' build'n high."

Lónae nodded her head and was about to speak, but Fendun was already turned, urging Andreno toward the trees. As they moved forward, Andreno's gait slowed him and Fendun had to check his steps. He dropped back impatiently to Reno's side.

"Lead, Reno," he urged.

CHAPTER 15
LIAM SPEAKS

In Andreno's absence, Jardán became the only guiding force for the people of Falmora. As he watched their practice from his high tree, Dan began to realize the lack of understanding in the Irelmen. Their movements were still too hesitant and scattered; finally, it occurred to him that the men on the ground did not share his advantage. Slowly, each day, Dan began to bring a few men up to the tree to watch the morning practice until all the Irelmen had viewed the activity from above. They began to grasp the importance of the movement of groups and the tactics used, and as each returned to their training, thoughts were focused on the larger meaning of their efforts. The Irelmen put aside their individual aims and gained a true understanding of tribe. They gained, too, a total trust in Jardán—unconditionally, he was their chief.

Along with belief in their leader, the Irelmen had gained confidence in their skill as warriors, for Farliam unerringly spotted and corrected the weaknesses in each man's technique. Farliam was so exact in pointing out shortcomings, and the Irelmen were so quick to learn and adapt, that soon Farliam became an observer whose advice was needed only occasionally. However, the Irelmen drew strength from Farliam's silent presence and they respected his knowledge and his willingness to teach.

In the evenings as the people gathered around the fires, they began to talk of their enemy and the impending battle. Inevitably, in searching for justification for their dangerous plans, they began to rely on hate.

"Thé be not like true kinsmen!" one young Irelman began.

"Aye," answered another, "Livin' North at th' open edge—no forest an' naught but bog an' low-growin' things to surround."

A young woman asked cautiously, "Whar be thé livin'? Be thar caves on th' moors?"

One of the young warriors who had been on the recent scouting party answered, "Aye, but bare few caves—thé be makin' false caves by stackin' o' stones!"

Quiet comments of surprise spread through the group. Then someone asked tentatively, "Be thé truly eatin' th' meat o' squirrel?"

No one spoke at first, then an older man said boldly, "It be thé way to break Havar's laws—aye, thé be eatin' meat."

A succession of outbursts answered from all directions:

"What one has seen th' eatin' o' meat?"

"Aye! Thé break all laws—Falmora canno' leave it so!"

"Havar spoke false! Thar should be no laws from such a one!"

"Aye, nor can trust be had from any such fair-haired!"

At this last, Neenah gasped and was on her feet in protest. "Thá canno' say so! T'were Reno—a fair son—that told o' Havar an' th' false laws!" Then, realizing she was standing up before all Falmora, Neenah sat down quickly in confusion.

Some nodded and some only stared at the ground, but all eyes followed as Jardán rose to speak. "It be true that Reno tells o' th' false laws o' Havar." Then Jardán looked around slowly to be sure they all were listening, "In what purpose be th' tellin'?" He paused briefly to let them consider the question. "Soon Reno leads all Irelmen to battle. Be it not forgot, when last th' Irelmen left Falmora, thé too followed men o' light hair—men o' Havar—an' ne'er be returned!"

A low rumbling of agreement started through the crowd and some were rising to their feet, when a strangled scream of protest rang out above all else—"Arrl!" Farliam walked quickly around the center fire shaking an upraised staff. He stared out at the dark cluster of people as he circled more slowly and declared, "Thá canno' make it so by false agreein'!" He raised the staff above his head, "Un marked as it be done—thá canno' change." Liam held out the staff toward the fire where the intricate slashes along its length were illumined by the flames.

Stunned by this sudden outburst from one whose voice had been silent so many years, all sank back to sit or squat low, and were speechless. What was it that Farliam was saying? Were his words clearly connected to his thoughts after all these years of silence? Out of the respect they held for his silent guidance in training, the warriors waited to hear him finally speak. Out of fear and awe at his face contorted in anger, the Irelwomen kept quiet to hear him. And out of caution in face of the unknown, Jardán held his tongue and watched Farliam closely.

"What ones be in Falmora in th' time o' Havar—an' afore?" As he spoke Farliam raced to the spot where he had been sitting and picked up three more staffs. Carrying them back to the fire, he stabbed one into the ground and ran his hand along the carved pattern of notches. "Here!" he exclaimed as his hand stopped on a particular groove, "All lived as brothers—light an' dark."

He stabbed another staff into the ground. "An' when Havar led all Irelmen from Falmora," his hand traced the notchings on the second staff, "what brothers an' what fathers followed? All! Be light an' dark leave as brothers—but none to return. An' what heart in Falmora stay still an' will not follow after those gone? What one here do not silent grieve for lost ones—light an' dark?

"All! All are grieved! How? Th' enemy o' Falmora come not from afar—come from Falmora. Half o' Irelmen sought to kill th' enemy not truly thar—an' could not, for th' enemy were by them an' with them."

Farliam slowly shoved the last staff into the ground. Only a third of the staff had been notched. He ran his hand along the smooth portions. "Do not weaken th' morrow nor make familiar an' not worthy by repeatin' th' pattern o' days gone. When Irelmen leave Falmora, know thá enemy! Not th' light-haired ones, but th' evil that brings notice o' light aside dark!

"When Reno leads, 'e leads aside Dan, brothers. When thá follow, follow as brothers, as Irelmen. Do not follow false in light nor dark. Do not be halv'd again by false purpose."

Liam's voice had softened now and his look had changed from anger to sadness. "Un wait to mark th' end—an' start anew. Mark th' path well. Quick carvin' an' hands not steady will give no fair pattern an' cause th' breakin' o' th' staff."

No one spoke. There was a small shifting of bodies and shuffle of feet. The wood popped on the fire and sent red embers shooting upward. Jardán stood at the edge of the firelight. His arms were folded across his chest and his eyes scowled. But as he looked around at the fire-lit faces he saw many nod, and some looked uncertain, but thoughtful. He cleared his throat to speak, then abruptly turned and walked away. The Irelmen watched his disapproval and were unsettled.

Farliam's body sagged as if the effort of speaking after so many years of silence had used all his energy. Slowly, he worked the staffs out of the ground, and gathering his things, he too walked away from the fire.

CHAPTER 16
ANGARA'S RETURN

In shades of black and brown, great naked limbs and trunks of the winter forest stretched upward toward the flat grey sky. All around the ground in twisted leafless profusion, the winter-bare undergrowth reflected the same hues. Random spots of dark lichen and moss kept a memory of color. And visible during the winter, as the land rose up to the highlands, dark patches of evergreen clung to the slopes of the mountains.

Among the tangle of winter brush by a small spring, Angara sat waiting, thinking. His arms and legs were gnarled and strong like the plants around him and his skin was weathered dark and lined from so many years spent without shelter.

Angara was very tired, but a feeling of deep excitement was surging inside his chest. He was sure that the events he had spent his life anticipating were fast approaching, He had watched the camp of Innismoor and although they were formidable, their strength was robbed by lack of conviction in purpose—there were many who were angry at Havar and many who had begun to secretly question his rule.

He had observed Falmora too. The warriors honing their skills and driven by the same revenge that had sustained him all these years. And they trusted their leaders: Farliam, so knowledgeable in the ways that men moved, both physically and spiritually; Jardán, a man who anticipated events and could view matters from afar; and, Andreno, a man of youth, honor and determination.

As he contemplated Andreno, he reviewed the events of the last two days. He had tracked Reno and his companions through the woods, careful not to reveal his presence. When it became clear that they would find Lónae and her mate, he drew back and waited, for there were many considerations for Lónae to face before he returned to her life. The lost father—or would she say the father who abandoned? Such thoughts of other's opinions had hardly entered his mind during his constant plot for revenge. In all his years of focusing on the wrongs brought by Havar, Angara had not given time to consider any wrongs brought by one man to his brother. Now that his goal was so close, Angara gave over his time to thoughts other than revenge. And most often they dwelt on his only ones: Fanáh, his mate; and Allialónae, his daughter.

In the past three weeks he had been in the woods, planning and deciding what his part in the coming clash would be. During his constant movement in the forest, he had been surprised and greatly relieved to find Lónae safe and living with a mate. The day he had spotted them during the snow storm, he had come much too close and had let himself be observed. His first thought in getting so close was to confront Lónae right away—but instinct had told him to wait. And now with the arrival of these new ones from Falmora, he was glad he had hesitated, for Lónae should resolve her new situation before she had to reunite with her father and hear of Fanáh's bravery in Innismoor.

Angara sat on a pile of dry leaves and twigs and leaned his forearms on his bent knees. He sighed loudly. He was not used to inactivity, but he could not think of one thing more he should do before he talked to Lónae—and that required a small wait. So he waited with the same determination he brought to every effort. He was so absorbed in his concentration to be patient that he was unaware of the sounds around him, and only knew he was being observed through some inner feeling which caused him to look up from his contemplation. There, very close, stood Tanéha regarding him with calm eyes. Her appearance was so sudden that he did not have time to react, and so he remained sitting and stared back. As he calmed from the surprise, Angara recognized her as the woman who had come to the woods with Andreno and Bandun. Unconsciously he nodded his head in recognition. Taking his movement as a sign, Tanéha stepped forward and raised her hand in greeting.

"How be thá here?" she asked cautiously.

Angara took a long heavy breath and rose slowly to his feet. He too raised his hand in greeting. "Angara. Father to Lónae, mate o' Anáh," he hesitated a moment, then decisively said, "Son o' Falmora."

Tanéha gasped audibly, then scrutinizing him, she argued, "Thá be not an ol' one."

Angara shook his head.

"Be thá banished?" she asked.

Again, Angara shook his head. Then he quickly searched his mind for a way to explain enough to gain her confidence. He asked, "Come thá from Falmora to seek o' one th' name canno' be told?"

"Aye,"answered Tanéha, perplexed at his knowledge.

"An' come thé too, Reno an' Dun?" continued Angara.

"Aye," noted Tanéha quietly, "How be thá know o' Reno an' Dun?"

"Dun, un be knowin' from young days in Falmora. Reno, un be knowin' from watchin' th' range o' knowledge an' darin'—an' watchin' th' trainin' o' warriors!"

For the first time she became leery of this strange man. Tanéha caught her breath and took a defensive stance, ready to fight even without weapons. "Be thá o' th' camp o' Havar?" she asked quietly, but demanding an answer.

"Arrl! " Angara raged. "Do not keep th' name o' evil in th' same breath with Gara," he said pounding his chest. "Un an' that one be linked on'y in battle—when un slay that one an' all that follow, in true avenge o' th' blood o' Gara an all th' ones taken down o' Falmora!"

The outburst frightened Tanéha, but she could not keep her thoughts still. "Why be thá here?" she asked, "An' not in Falmora?"

The question caught Angara off guard and a look of slight indecision crossed his angry face.

Suddenly, a voice boomed through the forest, "Néha! Whar be thá?"

Tanéha and Angara looked toward the direction of the voice and held their breath. Then Tanéha said, "'Tis Dun."

Angara tensed and felt a strange panic. Seeing his discomfort, Tanéha gave over to her instincts and stepped forward and lightly touched his arm, "Un believe thá speak true." Angara broke his gaze from the forest and looked into Néha's clear green eyes and he saw a depth not usually held in one so young. She continued, "Let Dun come to un an' thá." Angara nodded his head slowly and braced to meet the brother from his years in Falmora.

Tanéha called out, "Come thá this way!"

Within minutes, Bandun stepped through the trees to face them. He was so surprised to see the man beside Tanéha that for a moment he froze and just looked from one to the other.

Then he said, "What be th' meanin'?"

Tanéha started to speak, but Angara hushed her with a warning hand. He stepped forward, "Un be Angara. Mate o' Fánah. Father to Allialónae. Son o' Falmora."

For once in his life, Bandun was speechless. He remembered one named Angara from his boyhood, but that one had gone out as a boy with the men of Havar and had never returned. Angara would be gone, lost forever, like all the others—unless...

Bandun's face showed deep confusion; then he tried to cover his confusion by scowling at Néha, as if she were to blame for this new unknown.

Angara broke the silence. "Th' meanin' be many layered an' long in tellin'."

Bandun stepped in close, suspicion burning openly in his face. He held his long spear diagonally across his body, ready for defense. "Begin th' tellin'," he demanded. "How a son o' Falmora, an' ne'ermore thar? Whar be thá camp, an what ones in it?"

Hardened by his survival in the open and by his conviction of hate, Angara was not frightened by the aggression of any man. For a moment he looked at Bandun with disdain, disgusted by posturings in the absence of real danger. With great effort he controlled the insults forming on his lips and said instead, "See thá, un come not as warrior," and he turned his back on Bandun to show his complete lack of fear— and absence of warrior's knot.

Looking at the braided hair down the length of Angara's back, Bandun did not even have time to be offended by the gesture before Angara swirled again to face him.

"Soon it be so—when un slay Havar!" Angara shouted. His intense stare seared into Bandun, forcing him to believe. Willing himself to calm, Angara continued, "Come un to th' fire o' one that Reno seeks, an' further to Falmora. Un tell all what will be done."

He folded his arms across his chest and lifted his chin.

Bandun opened his mouth to protest the presumptions of the stranger, Angara, when a snapping twig made them all turn to see Andreno and Fendun step into their circle. Fendun immediately moved toward his father, but Andreno held him back with a warning arm across the chest.

Andreno looked warily at the stranger.

Angara's face reflected a glow of respect as he faced the young leader he had often watched from afar. Angara unfolded his arms and raised one hand in greeting, "Aruh, Reno."

Andreno gripped his long spear tighter and shifted his eyes over each of the faces to weigh for danger. He narrowed his eyes. "How be thá know un?" he asked.

Angara smiled and said, "Un know o' many things thá will know when all be returned to Falmora."

Impatient with the repetition of the conceited claim, and with Reno to cover the crazed stranger, Bandun could not contain his joy. Forgetting the insolence of the strange one who called himself Angara, and ignoring all danger, he dropped his long spear, rushed between Andreno and Angara, and threw his arms around Fendun.

Andreno warned, "Dun!" But it was too late. All caution had been broken and father and son were already clapping each other on the back in noisy reunion.

Trying to regain advantage, Reno moved closer to Angara and raised his spear. But Angara ignored him; his eyes locked on the reunited father and son. Suddenly, Angara threw back his head and laughed in pleasure—the raucous noise reached through the dry forest and startled birds into flight.

Bewildered, Andreno slowly lowered his spear. Bandun turned, still gripping his son, and indicating Angara, he said, "Be damned to crazed lost ones on such a day!" This made Angara laugh even harder. Angara's manner was so odd and his reaction to others so fearless that Reno sensed no real danger from him, and in the joy of reunion, he could not suppress his own grin.

CHAPTER 17
RECONCILED

The five that Lónae saw emerging from the forest made the largest group of people she had confronted in her life. She singled out Fendun immediately, walking beside one who must be his father. Behind them walked Reno and a dark-haired one in long skirts. But leading all was a solitary man whose bearing and coverings revealed him as the one who had stalked her in the forest. She stood up in confusion, then as the group drew closer, she recognized Angara and raced forward to meet him. Angara opened his arms and lifted Lónae, whirling her in circles.

Fendun had watched Lónae run toward them and had thought only of her approach to greet him. As she swirled now in the arms of her father, he stood with his mouth open in amazement—for he had missed Angara's explanations in the forest, and the group had immediately moved without further talk toward the cave after his reunion with his own father.

As Angara stopped his whirling, he and Lónae turned toward the others and saw Fendun's expression. His look was so astonished that it set off another peal of laughter in Angara and infected Lónae, and she too began to laugh.

Fendun's expression changed to bewildered anger and Lónae suddenly became aware that no one else was laughing. Still too delighted to feel uncomfortable, she pulled Angara toward Fendun. Taking Fendun's hand, she placed it with her's on Angara's forearm and announced, "Fendun, mate o' Lónae."

Now it was Bandun's turn to be astonished—and he looked on as the crazed one, without ceasing to smile, stepped close and embraced Fendun, then pushed away and roared, "Angara! Father o' Allialónae!"

There was an awkward but content meeting around Fendun and Lónae's fire as they prepared to travel back to Falmora in the coming morning. Since Angara remained the most recalcitrant and the least reserved, he plunged right into the telling of his tale. He began with his account of watching Havar's massacre of the dark-haired ones of Falmora, then through his secluded life in the forest with Fanáh and Allialónae, and concluded with his recent solitary scoutings of Falmora Glade, Havar's camp and the forest.

He limited his report of his stealthy observations, however, and ended by stating, "Un tell many things thá will know o' Havar when returned to Falmora. Un tell all in council what must be done."

At this statement, Bandun could no longer contain himself. He jumped to his feet and declared, "Thar be ones chosen by council to lead against Havar! People o' Falmora follow one Dan, one Liam, an' one Reno." As he said Reno's name, Bandun looked with pride at his son's brother-friend. But Reno stood up with a stern face.

"Aye, Dun. Thar be Irelmen to lead, but none be knowin' what Gara tells. Gara will speak at council, an' then it be decided what shall be."

Bandun's pride fed his anger. Incredulous, he asked, "Thá hear words o' one above the council? One that lives apart an' will not seek brothers?"

Reno's face showed no expression, but Angara held a slight smile.

Angered by the perceived insolence, Bandun continued, "An' one that teach th' way o' th' hunt to women..." he turned his glare on Lónae, "an' one what keeps silent as women speak as men, an' dress as men? An' live as quick-mate with no word o' th' council or blessin' asked?"

Fendun now stood to speak, guilt and anger warring for his will. But his feeling for Lónae won over all, and he spoke first for her. "Lónae lives not against th' way o' Falmora, but away from, not knowin'. Lónae's ways be o' one that survives, not in th' warm circle o' the council fire, but as one without brother in th' forest.

"Un, son o' Dun, live so, as one without brothers. Be it so that when un return to Falmora, un canno' speak at council?" His look challenged Bandun. Then his feelings for his father softened his voice and he added, "Un an' Lónae be mated by laws o' th' forest. From many days long in sorrow with lack o' brothers, two became as one. Thar be no council nor father to give th' blessin'."

Bandun closed his mouth with an audible clamp and sat down to think.

Listening to all the others, Angara's smile had faded slowly and now he rose to speak.

His voice boomed out, "Do not spend days in anger o' change an' diffr'nce that be no harm! Bring down th' great evil—that be our purpose!"

Bandun was not placated, but he fell silent. No one spoke again that night of any concerns. Angara had focused their thoughts well on Havar.

CHAPTER 18
FENDUN'S RETURN

Sentries sent word ahead to Falmora Glade of the approach of Fendun and his returning search party; and also word of the two strangers who travelled with them. But even so, the sight of the confident, weather-worn Angara walking beside Reno, and Allialónae with her streaming light hair, leggings and weapons following right behind, her pace matched to Fendun's, was rare enough to cause the people of Falmora to cluster in groups and stare—some whispering behind hands.

Bandun and Tanéha followed last. As Bandun saw the critical and suspicious looks aimed at Allialónae, his emotions twisted and he glared angrily at those who showed their disapproval. Suddenly, he was silently defending one who so recently he had criticized— Fendun's choice was made, so let none speak against his outcast son so recently returned!

When they reached the center of the glade, Reno immediately called for a council.

As the people gathered around, Farliam made his way to stand close to Reno, but Jardán stayed at the edge of the crowd and quietly positioned warriors all around the group. Reno spoke first, anxious to finally lift the burden of banishment.

"Un brother Dun returns. Thá be forgiven."

A loud murmur of approval rose up and some men nearest Fendun reached out and clapped him on the shoulder. Then there was an awkward silence and Bandun spoke up.

"'Tis a time o' celebrate, an' more un do not care!" Bandun heard a low sound rumble from Angara's throat and he glanced sideways to see Angara's angry gaze. Hurriedly he added, "Afore all, comes th' fall o' Havar."

In the crowd, Jardán jerked his gaze from Bandun to Angara, observing the subtle exchange and wondering at the sway of power. Alert, he watched the faces closely: Reno, Farliam, Bandun—and this powerful stranger.

A small sigh of disappointment flowed through the people, and Angara, angered by the sound shouted out, "'Tis Havar the evil one that must be slain—afore all causes other!"

The people quieted in surprise at the stranger's outburst, speaking out at council, not a Falmoran and not even identified. Some began to mutter their disapproval and the warriors at the edge imperceptibly moved in closer and gripped their weapons tighter.

Sensing the very discord he had feared, Fendun stepped forward quickly and spoke, "Un return as son o' Falmora. Un return with a lost one." Fendun stepped beside Angara and said formally, "Angara, son o' Falmora." Some of the people recognized the name and began to immediately speculate about his presence. But before the voices could get too loud, Fendun walked to Lónae's side, and taking up her hand he said, "Allialónae. Daughter o' Gara. Mate o' Dun!"

Everyone began to talk at once. Jardán started to push his way to the center to gain control. Lónae stepped closer to Fendun, and Angara began to scowl in impatience. Bandun was about to speak again when Farliam stepped forward and raised his staff and shouted, "Hold!" And the people silenced. Jardán was frantically pushing his way through the crowd, but Farliam continued before Dan could speak.

"Tis th' first o' many diffr'nces to come to Falmora. Thá must listen first an' then discuss. Let th' new ones tell a tale."

Just as Jardán finally made his way and stepped to the center, Angara walked forward and Jardán too felt the palpable strength of Gara's presence. Without further interruption, Angara began to speak.

He poured forth for all of Falmora his sad tale of Havar's deception and slaughter of the Irelmen and of his own hardship and resolve to avenge those who had died. He explained his isolated life with Fanáh and Allialónae, and their eventual dispersion with his most recent attempt to constantly observe both Havar's camp and Falmora.

As he spoke, the Irelmen listened with rapt attention and although they now knew of Havar's deceit, the re-telling of the story by one who had actually lived through it gave the tale a strength that made it finally and terribly true.

A pall fell over the silenced Irelmen as they absorbed the wrongs that had been forced on them. A wave of despair and stagnancy flowed through them and settled like a weight on their bodies. Even the warriors slumped in sadness at the thought of the destruction of good faith and brotherhood wrought by Havar. The intentional destruction of trust by kinsmen was a more incomprehensible loss than the actual death of their brothers at the hands of an unknown enemy.

Even Angara was affected by the people's reaction to his account and he was temporarily silenced, exhausted by the telling. Farliam and Jardán both recognized the danger of such a mood and the languorous hold it could have over the people. Jardán's eyes met Farliam's with a look of panic—the leader somehow had separated from his forces. Farliam nodded his head in understanding and said, "Speak thá, Dan."

Jardán's voice was sharp across the hushed people.

"Havar be still alive! What ones be stayin' in Falmora, leavin' th' squirrel meat to make Havar strong? What ones be sendin' th' old ones away to stop th' rememberin'? What ones will keep th' travels to two day's length by command o' Havar?" As Jardán spoke the people were gradually jarred to attention by each of his reminders and they lifted their heads, alert to his speech, until he finally said, "What ones follow th' rule o' Havar?"

And the people's answer resounded through the forest: "None!"

Now shaken from his own silence, Angara stepped forward renewed. He shouted, "Un an' thá go then—in two day's passed!" Anger flooded Jardán and he stepped next to Angara to reclaim his lead, growling to Gara, "'Tis too soon." Then he felt the collected energy of the people and saw the resolve returned to their faces. Instead of reprimand, he placed his hand on Angara's shoulder and called out:

"Two days—no more!"

CHAPTER 19
SUSPICION

A nd so, Fendun's return to Falmora was not marked by celebration, but rather by tense efforts to bring warriors and supplies together in readiness. As the council dispersed, each went separate ways in urgent attempt to complete preparations. The unknown ones, Lónae and Angara, were readily incorporated in any group efforts, but mostly left on their own.

Angara wandered in excitement from one cluster of men to another, giving enthused nods and encouraging comments. Lónae was strangely silent and withdrawn, staying on the edge of all activities, not a part of either the men's or women's groupings. She checked her weapons and practiced with the long spears and flying spears; but that was her usual daily habit and so it was completed efficiently in a short time. For most of the afternoon, Lónae sat in the glade inspecting her flying spears and secretly observing the actions of the Irelwomen. She watched as they moved, graceful but encumbered by their long skirts. She overheard their conversations about caches of food, conditions of weather, the adequacy of the skin supplies for clothing and pouches— and she sighed in weary disappointment.

At first, she couldn't distinguish what it was that made her uncomfortable about Falmora, the one place she had always wanted to be. Then, gradually, she realized that the company of her kinsmen brought restrictions of behavior. Lónae wondered if she would be able to accept those restrictions. At the thought of trying to move in skirts and giving up her weapons, of curtailing her walks through the forest and limiting her speech to follow that of the Irelmen at council, Lónae's heart beat fast in anxious fear, like any of the creatures of the forest when they are threatened. Her fair skin grew even paler and she trembled with nausea.

Although Tanéha was busy with the preparations for the warriors, she kept a vigil on Lónae. When she saw the look of fear cross Lónae's face, Tanéha hurried to the fire and poured a gourd of tea. As she offered the steaming tea, Tanéha placed her hand gently on one of Lónae's and said, "Thá be not sad. Dun be returned safe from th' battle. An' Reno. In th' celebrate, un an' thá be blessed by th' council for th' mating day. An' all lost ones be embraced by Falmora."

Lónae's hands shook as she lifted the gourd to drink.

Alarmed by Lónae's pallor, Tanéha reached out to brush her hand across the pale brow and felt the heat. "Be thá not well?" she asked anxiously.

Lónae's eyes filled with tears at the sudden gentle concern. Then immediately she brushed her eyes dry and stood up unsteadily. She put her hands on her hips and said, "No! Un be strong! Thar be no waitin' for th' return. Un go beside Dun!"

Tanéha stood slowly with a look of disbelief. "Thá be no warrior!"

"Un be more warrior than o' Falmora!" Lónae answered, then turned and walked toward the woods.

"Lónae!" Tanéha called and hurried after her. Just as the cool darkness of the forest enveloped them, Tanéha reached Lónae and touched her shoulder. Lónae turned and could not ignore the look of concern on Tanéha's face.

Lónae spoke more softly, "Un canno' on'y stay an' wait—not on this day. Do thá know tis so?"

Tanéha nodded her head sadly and Lónae reached out to brush her forearm in recognition of the kindness, then turned to go. But Tanéha called out again, "Lónae! 'Tis more un know!" Lónae turned back at the insistent tone. Tanéha continued, her voice lowered, "Thá be soon slow with weight o' th' child."

Lónae stood silent, astounded. Her first thought was of a trick, a way to stop her going; but just as that thought formed, a shiver of awareness went through her spine. She looked into Tanéha's deep green eyes, and she knew it was true.

In a barely audible whisper she said, "How be it thá knows?"

Tanéha answered, "Un know," she paused, searching for an explanation, "Un know, through th' heart." And she placed a fist over her chest.

Lónae accepted the explanation without question. She hung her head under the force of the thoughts crowding in. Tanéha waited, respectfully quiet. Lónae slumped against a tree trunk. She stared at the ground in silence for a long time. Then slowly, she raised her head and looked at Tanéha with shining eyes, full of renewed purpose.

Grasping Tanéha's hands, she said, "Thá will not tell Dun? Un will go to

Innismoor—an' celebrate all when returned!"

Tanéha was so surprised she could not speak. She stared with open mouth.

Lónae urged her again, squeezing her hands tightly, "Thá will not speak o' this?"

Tanéha began to shake her head in protest, but Lónae took the movement as an agreement to silence. She released Tanéha's hands and smiled.

"Thá be true kinsman!" she exclaimed, then turned and hurried away.

In the early evening, a strong wind began to blow. It could not pierce the forest Falmora, but the tops of the trees swayed and rustled and sent whispers of the approaching storm down to the very floor of the forest. In Falmora Glade, the wind dipped and howled as it hit the sudden open space amidst the dense trees.

The disquiet was reflected in the warriors of Falmora, as if the storm had entered their being. They moved nervously from fire to fire, checking their spears and supplies, talking briefly in small tense groups crouched around the wind-whipped fires, and staring often into the forest, toward the North. It was an evening to seek shelter, but the Irelmen felt a great pull to stay in the wind and keep watch.

Inside the very base of Jardán's tree, where the wind could not reach them, Reno and Farliam waited with Jardán. They would meet with Angara to discuss their final plans and methods of attack. Angara had already described the contours of the land and the arrangement of the camp of Innismoor, but Jardán insisted that Angara be present to point out any flaws as they talked through their battle plans.

As it grew late and Angara did not come, Reno went out to find Fendun and together they moved from campfire to campfire around the glade in search of Angara. They did not find him among the clusters of men and they moved quietly around to all the sentry posts to ask about any movements detected in the forest. They found no sign of Angara. Together, they sought out Lónae, but she had not seen her father since early afternoon.

With suspicion and dread building in their thoughts, Andreno and Fendun returned to Jardán. Angara had fled. As they disclosed their search and their suspicions, Reno and Dun watched a hard stillness overtake Jardán's face. Expecting a great outburst, they grew increasingly uneasy as Jardán made no move or sound—but only sat scowling. Fendun shifted his position restlessly and Andreno cleared his throat to speak, but Farliam cautioned him with a silent shake of his head.

Finally, Jardán drew breath and rose to his feet. Quietly he said, "Tell none o' this. Say on'y that Gara be gone afore th' Irelmen—to search th' path."

Andreno's eyebrows raised in question, but Jardán continued, "May that it be so—for Falmora will not bear a traitor. May th' night be th' dark tanned strip that binds all Irelmen as one, an' may th' light o' morn' not show that th' dark hide be stretched too thin an' far. A weak spot o' th' hide will be o' no use an' will be cut off!"

Without waiting for comments or further speculation, Jardán whirled and disappeared into the inner chambers of the great tree roots.

CHAPTER 20
MARCH TO INNISMOOR

Toward the middle of the night, the winds died and a soft rain fell. Andreno and Fendun sat huddled just within the forest at the edge of Falmora Glade. Except for the posted sentries, they were the only Irelmen who had not sought shelter and at least an attempt to sleep. The clouds covered any possible light from the moon or stars and the steady rain had extinguished all the open fires. The glade was a large black empty mass within the forest, softly undulating with the waves of rain, like the breath of a massive sleeping creature.

The total absence of light and the incessant rain kept each man wrapped in his separate coverings of fur and forced their thoughts inward. Both were anguishing over the possible motives for Angara's actions. Andreno drew both comfort and uneasiness in the thought that Angara kept one purpose above all else: revenge against Havar. That purpose would surely keep his actions true—but at the same time he had sworn no allegiance to anyone, and his actions might bring harm to Falmora.

Fendun drew little comfort in considering Angara's actions, for he could not help remembering his conversation with Lónae about how a man determines what actions are right; and Fendun knew that Angara strictly followed the urging of his heart.

As the two stared out at the blank darkness, a darker form was just discernable against the black backdrop of the glade. It moved slowly in their direction. Reno and Fendun stood up cautiously. As the form came close, a voice called out softly, "Reno?"

Andreno relaxed at the sound of Tanéha's voice. "Aye," he answered.

Tanéha rushed forward and clasped Reno. "Thá must go," she said.

Taking her statement as a question, Reno answered gently, "Aye, Néha. Un go when one night more be passed."

"No! Thá go now!" Tanéha almost shouted. And both Reno and Fendun jerked involuntarily at her tone. Fendun, who had discreetly turned his face away, even in the dark, as they embraced, now moved close to them and squinted intently toward Tanéha.

Reno spoke first. "Thá have seen Gara?"

Tanéha answered, "Un do not speak o' Gara. Un heard th' great night bird—th' sound o' flight pierced ev'n through th' rain—an' un know." Before they could object, she hurriedly continued, "Thá must hurry through th' night an' lie hidden by day. Thar be danger in waitin! Th' great bird does not wait, but strikes with night cover an' does not fail."

Reno was struck silent, trying to think through Tanéha's words. Tanéha, who desperately did not want Reno to leave, but who had become resigned to his going, was now seeking him out in the darkest hour of night to beg him to go immediately through the rain. It made no sense—then, suddenly, it made all sense as Andreno recalled the many times when Tanéha had confided in him about events she suspected, which later became reality. And he thought of her uncanny ability to heal with herbs. Had she not even healed his own life-threatening wound? And he believed in the power of Tanéha's knowledge and calmly and totally accepted her words.

Reno's words broke the silence, "Aye," he said, "Un go to tell Dan." Then, realizing the difficulty of explaining to someone who did not know Tanéha well, Reno added, "Be it that Dan may not agree."

Then Tanéha shocked them once more and said, "Dan be ready afore thá."

And as they made their way to Jardán's tree, they found him awake and fully dressed. By the soft light of the small inside fire they saw all his supplies wrapped and his spears bundled on top. Since Angara's leaving, Jardán had been unable to rest. He had checked and rechecked his bundles and impatiently waited the appointed day. Now as Andreno and Fendun came to him and suggested immediate departure, he took only a moment to consider, then ordered, "Bring all Irelmen unto th' glade."

Within a short while, all the warriors were assembled in the glade, bundled against the steady drizzle. Around their outside edge stood small, sad groups of those who would stay behind. The rain fell on all the faces and mercifully hid their tears. All were silent. When Jardán spoke, his voice rang out across the black glade, and gave words to their deadly actions.

"Warriors o' Falmora will go by night an' take cover by day. When th' moors be reached, take word o' what be done an' follow on'y Liam, Reno, an' Dan." They heard him pound his fist on his chest as he said his own name. Then he continued, "'Tis not for Irelmen to be returned to Falmora afore Havar an' th' evil be killed! Cling strong to th' purpose an' return as Irelmen free o' all false rule!"

He gave no words of comfort—for there were none. Now resigned to their cause, the warriors of Falmora turned as a group to the North and silently dispersed into the dark forest.

At the first sign of daylight, the warriors found sheltered cover and lay silent and bundled, for the rain continued in steady drizzle through the first day. By evening, the rain had ended and they were able to travel faster by the light of the three-quarter moon. They walked in silence trying not to think too far to the future, but aware that they moved ever closer to events that must hold their fate. They paused once at midnight to rest and eat, but dared not light a fire for they were approaching too close to Innismoor. By dawn of the second day, they took shelter among trees that grew noticeably more sparse than in the heart of Falmora forest. They knew from Angara's descriptions that the trees would soon thin to the open moors and their cover would be gravely reduced.

As the warriors sought out temporary shelter, they shed their outer skin coverings, for the day was clear and sunny—truly a first spring day. Jardán had warned them against unnecessary noise and talking, and they settled to rest so quietly that the bird songs at the top of the trees seemed very loud. Suddenly, a surprised cry rang out and the birds were silent. Instantly, everyone was up, weapons in hand, looking toward the source of the outcry and moving cautiously toward it. As Fendun made his way toward the sound, he saw a small group gathering; and as he and the others reached the group, he pushed to the front and his heart fell.

Standing in the center of the men, was Lónae. Her thick long hair was pulled back and carefully knotted as all the other warriors. She stood alert with her head high, but would not look anyone in the eye. As Jardán pushed to the center, the warriors broke their shocked silence and began raising protests all at once.

"Be silent!" Jardán hissed and the grumblings ceased immediately. In a harsh whisper, Jardán demanded, "What be th' meanin'?"

Lónae spoke low and they strained to hear, "Un go to Innismoor."

"Thá canno'!" exclaimed Bandun. His fierce disapproval of his son's mate was mixed equally with a growing protectiveness, and in his confusion he had screamed the words. Jardán jerked his head toward Bandun with a searing glance and Bandun clapped his hand over his mouth, but his eyes burned in angry frustration.

Fendun had made his way to Lónae's side and he shook his head sadly.

"Thá should not be here," he whispered.

Jardán glared at them both. He turned and stomped through the crowd of men, then swirled and stomped back to face them. Standing very close, he seethed at Lónae, "Thá be wrong to follow—but tis too long to send thá back." Turning to Fendun, he ordered, "Thá be th' guard o' this woman. Hold Lónae apart from th' battle!" Then turning to the warriors he fumed, "What warriors cling so in one group? Thá will be swept up in one blow! Have thá lost th' trainin' afore th' battle begins? Spread out! An' keep thá silent!"

Quickly the warriors returned to their places and Jardán turned away to check the sentries. Lónae put her hand on Fendun's in silent plea for understanding, but Fendun could not bear to look at her and risk her seeing the fear he felt for her. He turned and led the way to shelter where they lay silent, resting through the bright day—waiting for darkness.

CHAPTER 21
HAVAR WAITS

On a small rise a short distance from Innismoor, Angara lay hidden in the thick heather. As he watched the activity of the people and noted their routines, for the first time he was conscious of the presence of women and children in the camp and his mind struggled with thoughts of their possible death. Until this hour the thought of innocents being killed had not occurred to him. And now, within a day, or less, they might be slaughtered.

The full consequences of his need for revenge had never before weighed on Angara, and with the revelation, he lowered his head to the ground, burrowing his face in his arms. But as he lamented the sorrow to come, a memory came to him of a day many years ago when he lay hidden, watching, his body shaking with grief and fear. On that day he had watched as the Irelmen of Havar turned on their kinsmen and no mercy was granted. Angara saw again the turning of the fair Irelmen, their spears raised in sudden attack. His heart raced as he remembered the looks of astonished fear on the faces of the dark Irelmen. Once again, he saw his own father seized by the hair and bent backward while a short spear was pulled quickly across his neck and a great red spring of blood emptied his life. He remembered watching, paralyzed, as his father lay very still, the bright blood soaking into a dark wet patch of this stark treeless ground.

As the memory crowded his thoughts, Angara felt the same rage that had seized him on that faraway day. He looked up and searched the stone dwellings of Innismoor again. And he focused on something his eyes had overlooked. On the perimeter of the settlement there were tall piles of stone, built up at equal distances in a great circle around the whole of Innismoor. Angara's heart hardened. Here was solid proof to the guilt of the fair Irelmen of Innismoor—for what other need would they have of such monuments, than to hide behind in expectation of an attack? Angara's resolve was set once again. He quietly inched his body backward along the ground until he was far enough away to rise up and run.

He would carry news to the warriors of Falmora one last time.

Through the dark spring night the men of Falmora walked silent and tense, listening for any noise that might signal an intruder from outside their ranks. They moved carefully and slow, for they were very near to Innismoor and in the hour before dawn they would bring their hate and frustration into action, sweeping in surprise revenge upon Havar and any who chose to follow him.

At the point where the sparse line of trees gave way to the open moors, Jardán gave the signal for all to move forward by crawl. As he watched the dark forms ease to the ground, Jardán saw movement weaving through the prone warriors, crouching toward him. As the man came closer, Jardán felt the full danger that the open space presented; he squatted to the ground and held his long spear ready, balanced over his shoulder.

But as he watched the approach, something seemed familiar about the figure and he eased his grip slightly, trying to peer closer through the darkness. Then quickly, the man was beside him and Jardán recognized Angara's wiry form.

Jardán grabbed Angara's forearm in a grip that was more a warning than greeting. Both men stood, their muscles tensed, ready to fend the blows of close combat. Then Angara leaned forward and whispered, "Un come as kinsman. Take warnin' on'y o' th' news un carry."

Jardán held his grip as doubt flooded him. Then a movement at their feet caught his attention and Farliam stood up beside them. Farliam spoke in urgent whispering, "Do not kill for doubt—Gara be one o' Falmora!"

Still, Jardán held his grip and Farliam felt the two men tensed, neither able to speak. Farliam hissed, "Th' hour o' battle be upon th' land soon. Then will true kinsmen be proved—not here in th' blind grip o' two warriors bringin' death afore its time!"

Jardán stood silent, then slowly loosed his grip. The three stood so close each could feel the brush of the other's breath across his face. Without a word they lowered themselves to squat in a tight circle and Jardán whispered, "Speak. What warnin' be thar?"

Angara leaned in close and said, "Havar prepares for battle."

Jardán grabbed Angara's arm and seethed with hatred.

Angara continued urgently, "Not by un tellin'! Havar prepares for revenge to come—'e does not know when t'will come. Hear an' be warned, thar be great pillars o' stone strung round th' whole o' Innismoor, an' well placed to serve as shield for those that will defend."

Jardán sank back on his heels in thought, but did not contemplate long. Suddenly, he sprang forward with his powerful legs and with his face directly in front of Angara's, he warned, "If tis true—more need for haste an' surprise afore light!"

Turning to Farliam, he ordered, "Tell all o' this an' th' need to move without stop!"

Then, turning again to Angara, he said, "Un hear thá warnin' as true. Stay now an' fight as kinsman, for be thá gone when th' battles on—un will know thá as traitor an' un track thá to thá death. Be un dead—un spirit will rise up an' cause thá murder!"

Without waiting for a reply, Jardán turned and made his way through the warriors, stopping to give each the warning, and need for new caution and haste. Farliam and Angara moved quickly to spread the news and the warriors of Falmora hurried strong and silent through the bare darkness.

In the deep dark hours before dawn, Havar lay restless on his sleeping skins. The stone walls of his hut oozed with moisture and the peat fire hissed when trapped water was released by the heat. The skin flap across the hut opening hung still, unmoved by any night winds, and no sounds came from the camp of Innismoor. Yet, Havar struggled suddenly to his feet.

He cocked his ancient head—listening. There was nothing; but he felt something. Havar began to pull on his best outer skins. Using the walls as a guide, he ran his hands across the damp rough stone until he came to the opening. The stiff-tanned hide rustled as Havar pushed it aside and stepped into the waning night. The sentry turned toward the slight noise in silent alert, waiting for an order.

Havar stood silent and very still. His head thrust forward, his eyes squinted, but nothing seemed to move. A few campfires blinked red and yellow in the center of Innismoor; the stars had faded from the sky but the sun was not yet dawning. There was nothing to see. Nevertheless, Havar stood watching and listening. Slowly he reached just inside the hut and drew out his long spear, and waited.

CHAPTER 22
REVENGE

The Irelmen of Falmora slowed their advance in unspoken accord. They were very near to Innismoor. The scent of burning peat was in the air; and in the distance, small red glowing sparks along the ground showed the scatter of outdoor fires.

As they restrained their pace and crept ever closer to the ground, the warriors felt the lightening sky as if a dark weight were being drawn away in infinite slowness. Their hearts beat anxious in the still dawn, for soon they would be so close that even lying next to the ground would offer no protection, for the light would be full upon them. Each Irelman silently noted the dark shadows of the stone pillars and plotted a course of attack.

A gentle breeze began to blow and then abruptly it stopped. On the edge of the wind the night moisture was unsettled, and slowly from the deep crevices and low places a thick fog swirled swiftly over the land, obscuring even the hot glow of the dying fires.

The very air was held in thick suspension and the warriors froze in disbelief at their sudden fortune in the grey shield. Cautiously, they rose to their feet to advance. At that moment, a screech pierced the silence and the wing flaps of the great night bird echoed dully through the misty air.

In the front line of warriors, Andreno was jarred by the sound and instantly remembered Tanéha's prophesy of the great bird's wisdom. With no warning and oblivious of any command, Reno raised his voice in perfect primal pitch to the great bird's call and raced forward into the fog. The spell was cast, and the warriors of Falmora matched the piercing cry and were running into the attack with the atavistic instinct that always yields death.

And the sound that woke Innismoor was the hollow call of death. Unmistakable and immediate, the sharp cry was somehow familiar; as they opened their eyes to the opaque grey pre-dawn, the Irelmen of Innismoor knew with certainty that they had spent their lives listening for the wrong thing: for when the Great One calls you to your death, He does not use your full name—He sends a white and strident scream which signals your life's end and your return to the source.

The sentry warriors at the stone pillars were ready for attack, but in the blindness of the foggy air, the Falmorans were within the camp before a defense could be made. The rage and fog both caused horrible and unnecessary slaughter: mothers and infants were slain; the old and crippled fell in battle; children were victims—and in the confusion, the Irelmen of Falmora even slayed their own.

Desperate wails of anguish mixed with screams of hate and the sound of spear against spear rang out like strident tones of the underworld, while the dull thud of weapons striking uplifted shields kept a discordant rhythm.

The battle raged without plan until the sounds of combat grew less and less, and when the bright sun of daylight spread over the camp and burned away the fog—few skirmishes were left in progress.

Lónae had been wounded in her shoulder. She was weak from the fight more than from her wound. She stumbled between the fallen Irelmen in a daze. Suddenly, her eyes caught a glimpse of a familiar face and head, the blond hair strewn like wasted precious ornament along the ground in beautiful soft tendrils. Lónae stopped and stared at her mother. Fanáh's outer hides had been shredded from her body and a spear wound in her chest spread bright red blood across her pale naked skin, where it trickled across her ribcage and dripped dark spots into the earth. Lónae opened her mouth to scream, but suddenly fell to her knees and vomited. She sat back grabbing her knees and rocked herself slowly, mourning in silence.

Beside one of the central stone shelters, Jardán was in combat with one of the guards of Innismoor. Both warriors were tired, but Jardán's blows carried more force and he finally forced the guard to his knees. As Jardán raised his short spear high above his head to swing the death blow, a running figure caught his eye, and he recognized Angara—running for the open moors, away from the battle; and in the distance, racing to meet him were a fresh regrouping of Innismoor warriors, their blond hair glinting cold in the bright morning sun.

Angara's strides were swift and unfaltering as if running to join brothers instead of enemies. Jardán watched with burning hate. He flung his arms wide and screamed after Angara, "Traitor!" At that moment, the fallen guard regained his feet and slashed out at Jardán's sword. The swing missed its mark and fell instead on Jardán's upper arm, slamming it against the stone shelter. The grating sound of spear on stone signaled to Jardán what had happened, even before he lowered his eyes and watched his right arm fall heavy to the ground. Jardán slid slowly down the cool stones at his back, staring in disbelief at his own arm lying separated from him.

As the guard raised his spear for a death blow, a scream from behind him made him half turn.

"Arrl!" On short powerful legs, Bandun ran at the guard, with his long spear levelled. The blow was so powerful the spear went into the guard's abdomen and extended through his body, only stopping at Bandun's handhold on the shaft. Bandun released his grip and the wounded man fell sideways.

Bandun stared at Jardán's slumped form and at the severed arm. Jardán raised his head and smiled at Bandun, his eyes bright with shock. Bandun fought a rising nausea and said, "Thá canno' die, Dan!" And for a moment, Bandun stood wringing his big scarred hands like a child. Then an instinct deep within him caused him to grab Jardán around the chest and drag him to a campfire. With tears rolling down his face, Bandun pushed the bloody stump of Jardán's arm into the coals.

Jardán screamed and his whole body shook, then he turned unbelieving eyes on Bandun and fell back, unconscious. Bandun gently dragged Jardán to the shade of one of the huts, then stood slowly and his eye caught a movement on the moors that had been blocked from

Jardán's view. Across the open space, moving in slow but determined pace, the old ones of Falmora advanced with upheld shields toward the re-grouped warriors of Innismoor. And far in the lead, urging them on in his reckless solitary charge, was Angara.

Bandun swept his gaze quickly over the encampment and began running through the carnage yelling, "To th' moors—to th' moors!" Those warriors who were still standing jerked their gaze toward the moors and immediately understood the shift of the battle.

Fendun had already gathered warriors at the far edge of the camp behind Havar's lone shelter. Just as he was about to order an advance straight on, Fendun stopped and gaped as he watched the front line of Innismoor warriors drop to their knees. Then in one accord, all the men of Innismoor drew back bows and sent a hail of flying spears directly at the old ones. The old warriors lifted their shields and fended many of the spears, but a few fell wounded. Angara was directly in line and he fell, countless flying spears piercing his body.

Fendun shook off his surprise and ordered the Falmorans to circle behind. As they approached, Fendun's warriors too used their flying spears. The angle of attack caught many warriors of Innismoor unprotected, and as the survivors turned to face the new onslaught, the old ones advanced and caught them in close combat.

Andreno watched the final fight in sorrow and anguish. He winced as he dragged himself away from the bodies around him and managed to prop his upper body against one of the stone shelters. Both his legs were gashed and bleeding, and there was a deep puncture in his forearm. He felt lightheaded as he gazed out across the bloodied, littered camp. Like a dream, he watched two figures move toward Havar's shelter. The first was bent over with age and a cloud of yellow-white hair grew out of his large skull at odd angles. He stumbled as he groped through the opening. He was immediately pursued by a taller, sinewy man who grasped his weapons in one hand, and a large carved staff in the other.

At the sight of Farliam entering the shelter, Andreno closed his eyes in relief that one of those he loved had survived. He kept his eyes closed because he began to feel very tired. He began to feel that he was dreaming and he longed to stay utterly still and sleep.

Then loud shouts came from the shelter and disturbed his dream. The first voice struck his eardrums and sent a shiver through his soul:

"Un be th' Great One!"

It was answered in fevered hatred, "Thá be damned!"

Then the sounds of life tearing at life began—the sounds that had filled the encampment for the eternity of time that it took the sun to rise over the scene.

Andreno clamped his hands over his ears and screamed a silent scream. He opened his eyes and saw the red-black blood and gore and mangled beings lit up by the bright sun of the new morning. He saw a pale slender woman dressed in a man's leggings, her blond hair streaming loose all around her; and he watched as Lónae pulled aside the skin flap and entered Havar's shelter.

A scream rang out so filled with torment that Andreno knew he could not have dreamed it. With aching arms he pulled his torn body painfully toward the shelter. As he crawled through the opening, his eyes watered in the dim smoke, and slowly focused. Farliam lay in the dirt, his throat slashed open. On the ground beside him, Havar lay with a short spear through his heart. Lónae stood above him stabbing her spear into Havar's body over and over in slow rhythm. Each stab would catch in the body and Lónae had to jerk the spear free, sending a false shudder through the grotesque form.

'Lónae!" Andreno called. But Lónae would not hear him.

She kept at her slow, methodic stabbing.

Andreno pulled himself to where Lónae stood, and grabbed her legs. She fell heavy to the ground and began to struggle. Andreno crawled forward and grasped around her body, holding her arms down.

"'Tis dead. 'Tis th' end," he whispered hoarsely.

Lónae fell limp in his grip and began to wail in grief. Andreno looked again at the death beside them, and recognizing his father, Andreno sent out a wail to cover Lónae's and screamed, "Cease!"

As Fendun led his victorious warriors back toward Innismoor, Andreno's cry brought them first to Havar's hut. There they found their slain silent one, Farliam, his counsel forever lost. They found the almost unrecognizable form of Havar, never again able to spread evil. And they found the pitiful blond ones, clinging together in inconsolable grief.

When Fendun knelt to embrace his brother and his life mate, his lovely proud Lónae met his eyes with beaten spiritless gaze, while Reno looked up in delirious sorrow and asked, "Enough o' th' bright evil day—whar be un dream?"

CHAPTER 23
RETURN

The sad few who were able, began to tend to the wounded and drag away the dead. The ground of Innismoor was putrid with death, but even if it had not held physical repulsion, the place held an unseen force left by so many souls lost in violence. The Falmorans camped away from Innismoor that night and slept fitfully on the open moor.

As spent as they were, and even with many Irelmen wounded so badly they could not walk, each warrior yearned desperately to return at once to the cool shaded comfort of the forest Falmora. And so, within two days of the battle, the Irelmen began their return. Slings were fashioned of hides to carry the wounded. In slow silent steps, they moved southward, followed in quiet resignation by a cluster of grieving fair-haired women and small children of Innismoor who had nowhere else to turn.

On the day of their departure, the Irelmen were shocked to learn that the old ones who had managed to survive, intended to remain at Innismoor. Bandun and others protested that it bode ill and the place was evil. But, the old ones would not sway; and when the urgings of Fendun and the other young Irelmen went unnoticed, the Irelmen of Falmora finally shrugged in exhaustion and muttered that it was not a matter worth fighting.

Though some Irelmen were uneasy about leaving any living beings in Innismoor, others saw a possible meaning and use in the community of old ones; and, indeed, the wise and able old ones forged a powerful spiritual unit which gave them purpose and a longed-for companionship. They prayed each evening for the return of the next morning's sun to bring only light and warmth and never again the murder of kinsmen.

Hardly a word was spoken on the long trek back through the forest. Because of the burden of the wounded and because of their own exhaustion, the Irelmen stopped often to rest and eat. It was more than a full moon's cycle from the rainy night they had left Falmora until their sad return.

A few young Irel children playing in the forest first caught sight of the returning warriors and they raced ahead to shout the news. But, as the gathered Irelwomen watched the weary survivors shuffle into the glade, and as they saw how few had returned, a low keening wail rose up and the Irelwomen pressed forward—searching out the faces of the warriors. Many turned away, their throats constricting, horrified with the knowledge that the ones they waited for would never come.

Neenah spotted Bandun carrying the foot end of the sling that held Jardán. She hurried forward to meet him. Seeing her approach, Bandun held out his arms to her, unthinkingly dropping Jardán's feet.

"Arrl!" yelled Jardán. Bandun turned sheepishly to apologize, but before he could speak, Jardán was surrounded by Irel women, and his mate Myraynah, tending to his wounds. When Myraynah saw Jardán's arm was gone, she gasped and turned very pale, but she said nothing, for she felt full pity for those who would have counted the loss of an arm as nothing, if only to have their most-loved ones return.

Neenah patted Bandun's cheeks with her small wide hands and tears ran down her round face. She asked, "An' Dun?"

Bandun pointed across the cluster of people to where Fendun stood silently gripping Allialónae around one shoulder as they both looked down. There on the ground, Andreno had been carefully laid. He was still delirious, but Tanéha knelt by his side, quietly whispering to him and holding tight to his hand. Already she had sent some young ones to boil water for poultices.

As the practical matters of caring for wounds and building cooking fires were completed, Fendun looked at the groups around the fires and felt their unease. They had all looked in vain for Farliam, and even for Angara. Knowing what their absence meant, the Irelmen had looked toward Jardán, who was now caught in pain with half-opened eyes, and toward Andreno, still lost in fever. And now, they glanced repeatedly toward Fendun—waiting. Amid the expectant gazes, Fendun rose to his feet and walked to the center of the glade. No one spoke as he raised his hands to be heard.

"Many Irelmen—all brave and loved—be gone from Falmora. Thé be kinsmen all. Th' spirits o' th' lost ones be left on a broad an' open place—ringed with tall stone an' watched o'er by th' old ones that stay behind. Thar be too, th' souls o' ev'ry fair-haired kinsman. All lost."

A cry escaped from the small huddled group of women and children from Innismoor. The Falmorans looked at them in pity and then looked down in grief.

"Cease!" Fendun screamed and all faces turned to him, shocked.

"'Tis th' first order giv'n by un brother, Reno, at th' end o' th' battle, tis finished!"

Fendun snatched up the beautiful carved staffs that had been Farliam's and he carried them to where Andreno lay and placed them carefully on the ground beside him. Then he walked back to the center glade and continued:

"Let th' new wisdom hold! An' let thá look to th' ones left to remind thá." Fendun gestured at Jardán.

"Un see no diffr'nce here! " Fendun swung his arm and pointed at the sad group of Innismoor mourners. "Th' loss o' thé be not diffr'nt from th' loss o' thá! All kinsmen be lost! All be lost!"

Tears welled up in Fendun's eyes and for a moment he couldn't speak, but the hushed expectant people urged him on.

"Th' break be now mended—an' forever! From now, thá be all Irelmen, th' ones o' Dan—Tuatha dé Dannan!"

Fendun walked carefully to the place where Jardán lay propped up on a pallet of skins. He motioned to Bandun, who came at once with awkward short steps, balancing the burden of three great shields. The distinctive markings of each shield declared their owners and makers. One by one, Fendun lifted the shields from his father's grasp and laid them reverently at Jardán's feet: the shield of Angara, covered with the likeness of forest plants; the shield of Farliam, emblazoned with the intricate symbols of the stories of Falmora; and Fendun's own shield, etched with shadowy figures and strange animals.

Fendun said, "Lead thá now—un will follow!"

Jardán's eyes glistened and he reached out to grasp Fendun's forearm. Jardán gripped tight, nodding his head, and tears fell from his eyes. Seeing his father cry, the babe, Tunendan, began to wail. In the silence of the moment, all heads turned toward the little one and he abruptly shut his mouth and stared back at so much attention. Suddenly, everyone laughed at the child's innocence, and Fendun spoke again.

"Th' son o' Dan be near at one full year, an' not yet finish th' birth celebrate!"

Neenah needed no more mention than that. She immediately gathered the other women and they searched out the deep violet wines saved in the cool darkness of the great forest tree roots. As the Irelmen of Falmora drank slowly at first, and then with abandon, they had no heart for games on this celebration. But as they gathered closer around the central fire when evening fell, the warriors sensed a new beginning; and indeed, deep within Allialónae's body the promise of new life grew: twin sons, true brothers, yet one fair and one dark, two separate hearts beating in unison. The Irelmen heard the beat and each began to pound a rhythm on their taut war shields in unspoken release of the agony they had endured.

To the astonishment of all, in the absence of Farliam's telling, Tanéha sprang to her feet and lifted her voice in the story. Her's was more than just a telling, for her words glided together in a melodious meld in rhythm with the hands pounding their skin shields. Tanéha had brought song to the Irelmen. Her voice lifted the sad words of the battle and words of hope for the future high into the night where the notes wakened the roosting forest birds, and finally were dispersed and lost on the treetops. Tanéha knew that, now found, the song would not be lost, and soon Andreno would carve the story on the great wooden staff—the story of Falmora.

SIX STORIES

THE INDIGENT

"I have had a dream, past the wit of man to say what dream it was."
—Wm. Shakespeare

Clyde could feel the heat of the summer sun heavy against his body. There was a glow of light through his closed eyelids. Lying on his back he could feel the meadow grass softly mashing beneath his weight. In the brightness of mid-day it was hard to pick out specific sounds—the myriad of spring birds made up a crazed chorus of conversation. Yet the smells came through clearly: aspen bark, sharp-scented to match its stark-white color; wild flowers, delicate and almost imperceptible; the new grass, greeny-wet. Even the wind had the faint scent of pines from further up.

Clyde gave a huge pleased sigh and rolled to his side. He stretched out his legs and groaned with pleasure. Possibly, there was no better place anywhere than right here, right now.

Something began to poke Clyde's back. He squirmed a little to evade it. It poked in two places. Clyde jerked and sat up awake.

Suddenly the whole world was dark and cool. Clyde looked behind him in the dimness and saw Bernita's legs extended in sleep to where his back had just laid. He grumbled to himself and peered through the dawn light that was seeping inside. Even in the near-dark Clyde could see the mess around him. He could smell the rank stink of yesterday's food and the odor of bodies sleeping too long. His stomach felt queasy and that made his head hurt. And it all made him mad.

In a wrenching awkward effort, Clyde lunged to his feet and shambled noisily half-way out. Then he paused and looked back at

Bernita. She lay breathing heavily, her legs still extended. Her great heavy hips formed a lump that overshadowed the rest of her.

Clyde coughed and cleared his stuffy throat, growling out the congestion. Slowly he shuffled outside and stood squinting to see through the pale foggy mountain morning. The cold air of early spring made him hunch his shoulders in an effort to cringe his dirty matted old coat closer around him.

On an impulse he decided to hike down to the valley. He hadn't been down to see Jefferson since last fall before the snow.

At first he rambled in a wide zig-zag, not wanting to take the slope too fast. When the day grew lighter and he could see the small tails of smoke drifting up from the valley chimneys, he hurried his pace and began a straight-line descent.

By the time he reached the bottom he was running. Then he stopped abruptly and swayed slightly, deciding which way to go.

The valley was quiet and it was still early enough that no one was outside yet. Clyde walked along the foot of the mountain toward the stream. He slouched down on his belly and took a long drink. With water dripping down his hairy chin he sat by the bank and thought. He knew he shouldn't have come down. The people here didn't like his kind. Clyde's family and kin had lived way up in the mountains for years and the valley people looked on them as strange and even dangerous. Most of them were hateful to Clyde whenever they saw him.

But not Jefferson. Jefferson always talked to him. He always had something good to eat and he shared it with Clyde, even if it was through the back door.

Clyde's mouth began to water. He would just go to Jefferson's for a little something and then go on back up the mountain. He slunk through the bushes by the water, crossed the narrow dirt road and entered the nest of small valley houses. He was careful to walk fast and stay to the back of each house.

As he neared Jefferson's house, he looked around nervously to make sure no one was watching. Then he sauntered to the back door and half-heartedly thumped it.

Inside, Jefferson was sitting at the kitchen table drinking coffee and watching May cook breakfast. Amy was just walking in from the bedroom still in her pajamas.

"Mornin', britches," said Jefferson.

"Mornin'," Amy said reluctantly. She was six years old and didn't like her daddy to call her "britches" anymore, but she hadn't figured out a way to tell him yet.

"If you want breakfast, you better get some clothes on, girl," said May.

"Okay," Amy said and ran to change.

The knock was unexpected. May froze with her spatula in mid-air. Jefferson put down his cup with a slosh.

"Who could that be this early?" said May.

Jefferson stared for a minute. Then a slow smile spread. "Only one soul I can think of knocks at the back. Gimme a stack o' them cakes, May."

"Jefferson! You got no reason to feed that awful—"

"Now, Honey," Jefferson interrupted, "You know I never invite him in." He gave her a wink. "It does no harm. He don't hurt nothin'."

"But he could," she argued. "He's so big and he fidgets and acts strange."

"I'll just hand him out some cakes an' then I'll get him to leave. He doesn't like to hang around anyway."

Amy raced into the kitchen. "Can I come with you, Daddy?" she begged.

"Now you stay clear away from him, Amy. I don't want you havin' anything to do with him," said May.

"Oh, please. Can't I just once?" Amy insisted.

"I don't think it'd hurt if she just stood at the door, May," said Jefferson.

May folded her arms and shut her mouth tight. The knock sounded again. Jefferson stepped around his wife and stacked pancakes on a small plate, then motioned to Amy.

The two reached the back door at the same time. "Now you stay right inside and just watch," Jefferson whispered. He unlatched the bolt lock and eased open the door.

"Hello, Clyde!" said Jefferson. Startled, Clyde shuffled back a few steps. "Are you hungry this mornin'? We got plenty so I brought you out somethin' just in case you might be." Jefferson reached the plate out the door.

Clyde mumbled and edged forward a little. He darted his eyes at Amy, watching.

Jefferson sensed his nervousness and laid the plate down on the step.

"Here," he said. "I'll just leave it right here and if you want some I'll stay here an' keep you company while you eat."

Amy moved closer to Jefferson and watched as Clyde moved closer and sat right down on the ground. Using the step as a table he picked the pancakes up and shoved them into his mouth. Clyde sat chewing, spilling crumbs.

Amy stared. Then she whispered, "He seems awful hungry, Daddy, can't we give him something else?"

"Well," Jefferson considered. "Wait right here an' talk to Clyde. I'll be right back."

Amy looked at Clyde's dirty coat. She thought about how lonely he must get in the mountains. "Hi, Clyde," she said softly. "My name's Amy."

Clyde looked at her and scratched his nose. He craned his neck to look around her and into the house.

Jefferson returned walking stilted with a big mug. "Hey, Clyde, it's been so long since you've been down here, I thought you might want a little celebration drink. I got most of two beers poured in here. Try this out. My treat!"

As Jefferson set the mug out on the step Clyde seemed uncertain. He looked in the mug to be sure. Then decisively he drank it all in three big gulps. Clyde lolled his head a little to the side and burped. A bit of foam stuck to the corner of his mouth.

A door slammed next door and Alvin Whiters walked out the back of his house.

"Hey, Jeff," yelled Alvin. "We got some trouble hangin' around this mornin'?"

Clyde jumped at the sudden noise. He looked out the corner of his eye at Alvin, then anxiously at Jefferson.

"Guess maybe it's time to break it up, Clyde. Maybe you better go on now," said Jefferson. "Next time come by earlier."

"Hey! You been encouragin' him to hang around here?" Alvin yelled at Jefferson. He picked up a heavy stick from his woodpile and started toward Clyde.

"You better get on, Clyde," urged Amy.

Just as Clyde was heaving to his feet, Alvin hit him across the shoulders. Clyde groaned and staggered but managed to stumble sideways and started an awkward run.

"Git outta here, you!" shouted Alvin. "There's no sense givin' them an excuse to come down here," he glared at Jefferson.

Amy started crying.

Clyde made an unsteady run past the back row of houses. He looked back once and tripped over a washtub, sending it clanging a few feet along the ground. When he reached the mountain he clamored up in fits of stop and start until he reached home. Bernita was up, eating some of yesterday's leftovers. She gave Clyde a long hard glare. Clyde didn't care. His head hurt again and now his back, too. He eased himself across to the bed and fell on it. Bernita gave a disgusted snort. Clyde turned away from her and closed his eyes.

Within half an hour he sensed the meadow again.

"Stop that cryin', Amy," said May. "He has no business bein' down here anyway. Served him right to get run off."

Jefferson put an arm around Amy's shaking shoulders. "It's alright, Amy," he said. "Alvin hadn't ought to done that to Clyde. But ol' Clyde's strong and he wasn't really hurt. He's probably already home by now and relaxin'. Maybe even takin' a nap and dreamin' of spring!"

May gave Jefferson a hard look. "Don't be feedin' her tales, Jefferson," she said. "Any fool knows bears don't dream."

FONTRA

In the steamy warmth of the drain tunnel Fontra sat on the driest part of the ledge. Leaning over with his elbows resting on his thighs, he held his chin cupped in both hands and stared downward into the dark. The burble of the water was so soft he had to breathe very quietly to hear it. He remembered the strikingly constant small crash of woodland streams and his chest began to ache. The idea of the false stream running through a structured course of concrete below suddenly repulsed him. He leapt to his feet and began an urgent slipping run along the ledge toward the opening.

When he reached the long rectangular mouth, Fontra stopped very still and felt the fresh air rush against his skin. He stretched his neck to bring his eyes level with the rectangle and peered out to the pre-dawn. A pleasure of inward shivers ran through him. In swift movements he stepped up on the brick outcrop and pushed both hands high against the heavy metal disk, lifting it to one side. He pulled himself up through the hole and cautiously stood up on open ground.

A faint pink was mixing with the blue-dark sky and Fontra realized with dread that he wouldn't have time to run before daylight. Then he heard another runner coming. Instinctively, he crouched down to the ground.

As Erin approached the park she ran faster. It was darker running through the footpaths, but it was worth the small fear to run on something soft. Just as she raced the last length of pavement toward the trees, a dark shape moved low to the ground at the curb. A warm thrill of adrenaline pumped faster than her heart and Erin stopped. She stared, breathing hard. In the shadows the shape remained still.

A dog, she thought, and began a slow walk to skirt it. Almost opposite to the form, Erin realized it was much bigger than a dog. Then she saw his face—a man squatting by the curb. His eyes stared straight to hers in the dim light. She could see that he had no shirt on and long dark baggy pants.

Of course, she thought, *sweat pants*. Erin relaxed.

"Nice morning to run," she called and turned to move on. Then she saw him stand up and she sprinted toward the park. Behind her she heard a sharp ting with each of his footfalls. Through her fear the only thought that rose was: *Why is he wearing cleats?*

Erin could hear his breathing as they entered the park and within a few yards he raced beside her. She kept her gaze straight ahead thinking: *No one would hear me scream.*

In panic she panted, "What do you want?" and turned her head sharply at him.

His gaze was benevolent and he looked both amused and surprised. He answered, "To be strong—and healthy!" And he smiled at her with familiar communion.

His abrupt friendliness calmed Erin immediately. To parry his abruptness, she asked, "Why do you wear cleats?"

He cocked his head a little in question. "I don't understand?"

Erin said, "Your shoes. Why are you running in cle..."

Her voice closed off as she looked down to his feet.

She dead-stopped and watched his further paces. A long silken dark pelt grew to his body from the waist down—and his feet were cloven at the toes.

Fontra stopped and looked back at Erin. He followed her stare and glanced down at his legs, then gave a playful shrug with his massive shoulders and looked to the east.

"It's getting light," he said, smiling.

He moved toward Erin and she stumbled backward two steps, then jerked to her left and ran crashing through the trees. Behind her she heard a wonderful deep laugh.

Fontra stood watching and enjoying the hinder movement of her retreat.

Through the back door Erin stumbled into the kitchen.

She sat at the table leaning her forehead on her folded arms.

Gina shuffled into the kitchen in her fluffy chartreuse slippers. She finished tying her robe and sat opposite Erin, "Morning," she said, "or—just barely."

Erin lifted her head with a glazed look. "There was a faun in the park!"

"I guess that's the place they'd go," answered Gina. "But I didn't know there were any there."

"He was so big, though," said Erin. "I didn't know they were big."

"Maybe it was just a young doe," suggested Gina.

"He scared me," Erin continued, dazed. "But I don't think he was really mean."

Gina scowled at Erin and leaned forward, close to her face. "Is this some kind of new phobia? Fear of deer? Herbivore-phobia?"

"What?" asked Erin, listening for the first time.

Gina spoke sarcastically slow "Why did the deer scare you?"

"What deer?"

Gina looked exasperated. "You *said* you saw a fawn, and it scared you because it was big."

"Well, I guess he was more like a man. That's what scared me—at first—until I saw his legs."

"What?" Gina's voice rose. "You saw some man's legs in the park—at this hour? Oh my God! You're in shock that's why you're rambling."

Gina jumped up and came to put her arm around Erin, "Did he do anything? Erin, did he...? Oh...look, there's a twig in your hair. Did he knock you down? What happened, Erin?"

Erin leaned back a little from Gina's grasp and looked askance. "I'm okay. Nothing happened. I mean, nothing bad happened. Something *extraordinary* happened. At least, I *think* it did."

Gina released her hold. Erin leaned her chin on one hand, contemplating.

"You're a very sweaty person," Gina said with disgust, wiping her hands on her robe. "And not just a little strange, too. I think maybe you're having oxygen deprivation."

"Oh, Gina, I know how it sounds, but..." Erin stopped — suddenly aware of how it would sound.

Gina sat expectant.

Erin gave her a half-smile. "Umm, I don't know what to say. I'm not sure you'd believe me."

"Oh, sure. Okay. Now you don't want to talk. So why all the lurid hints? Do you want me to know or don't you?" Gina shifted impatiently.

"It's not that, Gina. It's just something so strange. I'm not sure myself." said Erin.

They sat in silence for a while.

"Look," began Gina," If you're meeting some guy at obnoxious-early-o'clock, that's your business. If you don't want to talk about it, that's fine."

"That's it!" said Erin. "I'll go back tomorrow and make sure. And, if he's there, I'll tell you all about it."

Gina wrinkled her forehead. "You mean you don't even know this guy'?"

"Well, no. Not exactly. We, um...met, but I'd like to find out if he's real."

"Oh, of course. We don't want any phony muggers running around in the park," Gina snipped.

"I'm sure he's not a mugger. He was real friendly," Erin explained.

"I'll bet," said Gina disgusted.

"Oh, Gina, that's not what I meant. Hey, just forget it for a while. I'll go see if he's there tomorrow and then I promise I'll tell you everything—so it makes sense."

"Do you think you should do that? I mean, go back there?" asked Gina.

"I don't know. Somehow I don't feel afraid," Erin answered.

Gina shook her head in disbelief. "Well, watch out for giant deer."

The next morning, Erin woke earlier than usual.

This is crazy, she thought—but hurried into her running clothes.

Her legs were shaky at first but after a few blocks she eased into an even run. As she approached the last block before the park she slowed to a walk. She stayed completely to the opposite side of the street when she came to the spot where she had seen him crouching. She squinted through the dim light. Nothing was there. She scanned up and down the block, but saw nothing.

Erin let out her breath. *Well*, she thought, *it's a good thing no one's here—I'm scared to death.* In relief she ran toward the trees. As she entered the footpath there was a slight rustle to her side. Fontra ran beside her.

Erin stopped. Fontra slowed and turned to stop. He smiled at her. Erin's mouth felt dry. "Is this a joke?" she managed to say, staring again at his legs.

Fontra smiled broader. "I like jokes," he said.

Erin relaxed a little. "I thought so," she said decidedly.

Fontra stepped toward her.

Erin bit her lip nervously. "That's a really *believable* costume. You fooled me right away."

Fontra moved closer. He stood next to her.

Trying to keep a conversation, Erin quipped, "How do you get that fur to stay on like that?"

Fontra laughed. "It's easy," he said.

Erin was reassured by his manner. "What kind of fur is that?" she asked. Unthinking, she reached out and touched the pelt at his waist. A shiver ran through Fontra's flanks, rippling the pelt.

Erin gasped and recoiled. "Real," she whispered.

Softly Fontra said, "You should learn to like jokes, Good jokes are rare."

Slowly he reached toward her. Erin stood paralyzed. Fontra carefully took her hand. He questioned her eyes. He smiled slightly.

"It will be light soon. Can you run very fast?" he asked,

Erin looked at his hand holding hers—gently, not against her will. She looked back to his face, now smiling broadly again. Slowly she smiled back.

Gina doesn't have to know everything.

ABSENCE OF MALICE

Smith is my very best friend and I wouldn't incriminate him needlessly but the fact is I think something untenable has happened. I've been an investigator for a long time— as long as Smith has been a scientist—and we've enjoyed exchanging details of our respective disciplines for over 20 years. But this time our disciplines have clashed.

I'm not going to say that Smith is crazy but I think it might be appropriate to say he's gone a little beyond eccentric. I've known a long time about his experiments and this is the first time he's actually hurt anyone.

I don't mean to infer that Smith is incompetent. He once worked for NASA on some velocity and trajectory problems. But in the last couple of years he has embraced some strange theories.

It all began several months ago when he was in the burnout stages of a project he called "The Earth as Terrarium." The original idea had religious overtones—or undertones—with the idea of life being "planted."

But it was the notion of the earth being *encased* that led him on to this new project. I don't know if he ever categorized it. You might say it began as the "Confounding of the Theory of Gravity."

The first premise in his theory was that space is *not* a vacuum but is composed of some matter which man has not detected, and that space actually has mass. The weight of space—according to Smith—presses on all sides of the planets, etcetera, and forms their rounded shapes and causes their heavier particles to cohere in the center. In a planet with an atmosphere such as earth's, the less-heavy objects such as people and animals are trapped between the pressure of the atmosphere and the hard surface of the globe and consequently cannot float around, but can move on the hard surface.

The second premise was that space is full of sound and if he discovered the true make-up of space, he would soon develop a receiver sensitive enough to pick up the sounds travelling around "out there." This premise sprung from the observed variations in speed that sound has through different mediums: 1,128 ft/sec through air at 68 F; 4,707 ft/sec through water at 46 F; and 16,000 ft/sec through iron pipe. Smith just deduced that since space is obviously heavier that iron pipe (from the first premise) sound must be travelling at an astonishing speed in space and he had only to figure out how to intercept it.

Naturally, this all led to experiments with ultrasonics.

Smith built a transducer—you know, those gadgets that turn sound waves into electrical impulses and vice versa. It's my opinion that this transducer has led to the demise of Smith's wife, Shirley.

But before I state my case, let me tell you about Shirley. She's been more than just a wife to Smith. She's been his lab assistant, bookkeeper, companion, and yes, guinea pig. I must make it clear that Smith would never intentionally endanger Shirley and through all their years of cooperative endeavors she has never suffered anything more serious than a case of dermatitis the time he held her suspended in saline solution for 24 hours, or the sprained wrist she got trying to clean his perpetual motion machine.

You should not form the opinion that Shirley is a chump—far from it. She's a very bright woman, but in whatever concerns Smith, she loses all awareness of common sense. She adores the man and will do absolutely anything to further his career.

Shirley is a tiny woman. In fact I'd say she's probably undernourished. I imagine she often just forgets to eat. She does try to maintain her health, though, and takes massive doses of multivitamins.

Last Thursday, I visited Smith in his laboratory. He had set up his transducer and was testing the effect of ultrasound on different materials. I spent the afternoon replacing material specimens and boxing and labelling the bombarded ones. That freed Smith to remain stationed at the microscope and jot down notes.

When Shirley came in from work I left for home. That evening Shirley was replacing samples in the target area just as I had done, when she—disappeared. Actually, the way Smith described it: he was looking into the microscope when he heard a loud "pop" and looked up to see a bit of floating fire which fell to the floor in a small heap of black soot.

There was no question about what had happened. Immediately despondent, Smith threw himself in front of the transducer beam—and nothing happened. Crazed, he ran upstairs calling out for Shirley and finally returned to the lab convinced.

He phoned me to come at once.

After listening to Smith's frantic explanation and examining poor Shirley's soot, I declined to step in front of the beam, though Smith contended that it was absolutely harmless. In desperation, he again stood in the impulse path and when I remained unwilling to try, he dashed upstairs and returned with the poodle and held her in front of the beam.

"See?' he shouted, "It *can't* have hurt Shirley!"

At that point he totally broke down and it was some time before I was able to talk to him. I urged him to think what conditions were different during the evening's testing. He assured me that everything was strictly controlled and the only variable was the material tested.

Well then, I reasoned, what was different about Shirley?

I ruled out the obvious male/female difference, not wanting to take a chauvinist approach—and taking into consideration that the poodle is female and remained unharmed.

Smith and I wrote out a detailed profile of Shirley. He supplied the details and I took notes. Smith was certain that she hadn't been sick or taking any drugs. When we'd finished, the one thing that stood out aside from her thinness was her massive ingestion of vitamins.

We both went to work on the facts. After two days, with our combined efforts, the conclusion we have reached is the only one plausible. Smith discovered that ultrasound is used in a metal removal process called ultrasonic machining in which high-velocity particles can actually wear away at a metal mixture to isolate the desired metal.

Shirley was probably in a dehydrated state. B-12 was among the vitamins she took. It is the only known vitamin that holds an ion of metal—cobalt—in its molecule. Cobalt is a very interesting metal. It's used as a catalyst in forming many ore alloys. Usually, it is a relatively inert metal, but finely divided, cobalt ignites spontaneously. The impulses from the transducer must have worked on Shirley's dehydrated cells, machining away until the fine particles of cobalt were released. Those particles mixed with the oxygen in her blood and— Pow!—they ignited.

Of course the explanation of what happened is small comfort to Smith. He ranted for several days to take him down to the station and charge him with murder. But I told him that one needs evidence, or a body, or a witness. I'm sure the deed happened—but without malicious intent. Am I obligated to try to explain to the DA? I think not.

I helped Smith carefully scoop Shirley into a graduated cylinder.

She remains in the laboratory close to his desk. She would have liked that and it seems to make Smith feel better. He's even tentatively talked of starting a new project: the conversion of molecules, I hesitate to speculate on the purpose of such a project or on the ultimate outcome.

CONSTERNATION

Light drizzle fell as the dirty tan station wagon pulled out of the gravel drive. The rear section of the car was piled to the ceiling with cardboard cartons, blankets, camp dishes, canned food, and house plants. The luggage rack was stacked with suitcases and extra boxes of clothes covered over with a black plastic tarp tied with twine. The load made the rear ride five inches lower than the front of the car, like some suburban "low rider."

Inside the car the faces of the Stengis family reflected the dark mood of the weather. In the front seat Lee Roy and Beth stared straight ahead, set already toward their destination.

Ellen Sue and Joe Bob sat low in the back seat. Each gave a last long stare back at the old house, craning their heads around until they could no longer see the empty windows staring back at them. At their feet, Big Boy meowed from inside his box with uneven dry gasps.

"You sure that movin' truck packed my new bike?" asked Joe Bob.

"Your Momma watched 'em load every stitch, Joe Bob," answered Lee Roy. Big Boy gave a loud yowl. "You git that cat ta stopper up its yawlin'."

"He's scaired, Daddy," said Ellen Sue. "Cain't we let 'im out now?"

"If that'll hush 'im up, you do it. But I don't want no messes in here."

As Lee Roy turned the car onto the highway, Ellen Sue pried the lid off the box. For a minute Big Boy cowered down in one corner and blinked. Then, like a huge furry spring, in two leaps he hit the back seat and bounced off, landing on the back of Lee Roy's head.

"Yeeee gads!" screamed Lee Roy. He jerked the car to the side and hit the brakes, lurching the luggage out of the rack and over onto the hood.

Big Boy loosed himself from Lee Roy's neck and lunged to the dashboard. He lay there panting - swishing his tail.

"Dang!" Lee Roy hit the steering wheel with his fist. "Git that cat! Git that dang cat. He's goin' in the back."

"But Lee Roy, it's full. The back's packed clear full," said Beth.

"Well move somethin', then. You move 'im back there in that box an' put a blanket over 'im."

"But he'll smother," whined Ellen Sue.

"It's yer own fault for lettin' 'im out," accused Joe Bob.

Lee Roy scowled at Joe Bob.

"Sonny," he ordered, "you git out here an' help put back these cases,"

As Joe Bob helped retie the tarp, Ellen Sue and Beth captured Big Boy and put him back in the box. By moving all the house plants to the middle of the back seat they were able to squeeze Big Boy's box into the back end and lay a blanket over it. When the car engine started, Big Boy began a muffled yowling. Ellen Sue looked back anxiously.

"He'll be alright," said Beth. "He's got air holes enough to breath."

Ellen Sue did not look convinced. She slumped her head against the door and looked sideways out the window. Beth glanced at Joe Bob's glum face.

"Well!" she chirped, "We sure got started off with a bang!"

No one said anything.

"Now look here," Beth's voice changed to lecture tone. "Y'all got no cause to sit moonin' back there with mean faces. Your Daddy's new job is an *opportunity*. From here on we'll be forward lookin' with no regrets."

Joe Bob and Ellen Sue squirmed and tried to avoid their mother's eyes.

Beth softened her look.

"Here," she said, handing the roadmap to the backseat, "why don't you try to trace our way on the map."

Ellen Sue and Joe Bob each held an edge of the unfolded map and gazed through the tangle of plants between them. Their eyes moved from the little envelope shape of Tennessee, tracing up and right to the irregular shape of New York.

"New York City has more people 'n the whole state o' Tennessee," Joe Bob announced.

Ellen Sue leaned forward around the plants suspiciously.

"Oh, that cain't be true."

"Yessir!" claimed Joe Bob. "I learned it at school."

Ellen Sue grimaced at him, exposing her full set of braces.

"Metal mouth," whispered Joe Bob.

"Momma!" complained Ellen Sue.

Beth turned sideways in her seat. "You two get on better. We got a lot o' travelin' to do. There's gonna be some differences where we're goin'—but it's not somethin' to fight about, it's somethin' to learn about," said Beth.

The car pulled into a gas station. Lee Roy got out to check the tires. Beth dug in her purse for change. "I'll get us all a pop," she said as she slammed the door.

Ellen Sue glanced toward the back of the car.

"I maybe oughta see if Big Boy's okay."

"Ah, he'll do okay," answered Joe Bob. "He'll be gettin' along better 'n you will once we get there."

"Whatcha mean?" asked Ellen Sue.

"Well," Joe Bob looked around cautiously, "There's some things about the North that Momma didn't mention—about all the people." He waited dramatically.

Ellen Sue looked uncertain and then brightened.

"Oh," she said," I already know about not sittin' down on the toilet seats an' stuff."

"Nah, dip brain," said Joe Bob, "I mean about the differences in the Northerns—like how they *talk*. They probably won't understand anythin' you say an' you'll have to start all over in school till they can figure out where you belong."

Ellen Sue looked worried.

"And them braces," Joe Bob paused. Ellen Sue ran her tongue over the sharp metal pieces in her mouth. "They won't understand how the old dentist wired 'em 'cause each place does it different. An' they'll get so mixed up when they tighten 'em again that they'll pull 'em all the wrong direction an' all your teeth'll start stickin' out every which way."

Ellen Sue's face began to cringe into a crying pucker. Then she glanced at the window beside Joe Bob's seat and sat up straight. Joe Bob followed her gaze and turned to see Beth stooped down at his window with two cans of Coke framing her scowling face.

Joe Bob slid down in his seat. Slowly he rolled down the window.

"Take this, J.B., and hand one to your sister," Beth ordered.

As they drove out of the station, everyone was quiet.

Suddenly Ellen Sue blurted, "Momma, will I still be in fourth grade when we get there?"

Beth turned to give Joe Bob a stare before she answered, "O' course you will, Ellen Sue. Most things'll be just the same. You two want a last look at Nashville? You keep your eyes open 'cause we're comin' close now."

As the highway narrowed to two lane city streets and the traffic slowed, they passed five men standing on the median strip handing out pamphlets. Lee Roy refused to accept the paper thrust through his window. Slowly the car edged forward and passed the men. Joe Bob and Ellen Sue stared back at them. Through the bobbing philodendron Ellen Sue watched the men. They looked like nightmare ghosts in their flowing white robes and stiff pointed white hats.

"Daddy," said Ellen Sue," Do they have the Klan up North?"

"No, honey, they don't," answered Lee Roy.

"Good." Ellen Sue settled back in her seat.

Lee Roy smiled and stepped harder on the gas as they moved out of the intersection.

THE INHERITANCE

My mother stopped talking to me when I was five years old. Thereafter, she would address me from time to time with the comment: "You're too much in thought about things. You're too tender-hearted." This reticence on her part did not stem from any harsh feeling, nor was she recoiling from the natural flow of inane or embarrassing conversation that young children tend to—it didn't bother *her* to be asked: "Why are there hairs in your nose?"

What bothered my mother was that I saw into her soul. I don't mean only that I knew her moods or habits—I mean exactly that I saw into her soul. The effect on our relationship was to cause my mother to consider me with suspicion and, what I didn't recognize at the time, with fear. I in turn felt a sense of shame and inadequacy for whatever unknown crime I was guilty of. As a result, I was always seeking forgiveness and approval. I remember leaving my kindergarten class in the middle of lessons and walking home just to see if I would be welcomed. But, that is trivial and not what weighs on me. The fact is: my mother was justified in her fear. I have just learned from my Aunt Evelyn the source of that fear.

Aunt Evelyn is mother's older sister. They've been dear to each other since the day mother was born. Evelyn was nineteen. She still calls mother "baby" though both have passed middle-age.

Before last week I had seen Aunt Evelyn only twice in my life. Years ago she eloped to the West coast with a Chicago gangster and never returned to the plains. She received me in her house as a child and as an adolescent—both times in the company of my mother. On those occasions, I was never allowed to talk to her alone but I was treated with extreme deference.

Her house hangs on a steep slope in the San Gabriel Mountains. There are lemon and avocado trees in the back with a profusion of aggressive flowering plants surrounding the sides and front. Pathways lined on both sides with giant sea shells run in a maze among the plants. The exterior of the house is a weathered wooden bungalow. Inside is a mesh of exotica and clutter. Two Amazon parrots have free flight through the rooms. An authentic Tiffany lamp hangs over a beat-up television with a bouquet of plastic flowers on top. Sterling silver spoons and Irish linen napkins sit on a cheap wooden kitchen table draped with a cracked vinyl cloth. The entire decor is an incongruity.

There is one room that serves solely as a storeroom for the overflow of trash and treasures. During my childhood visits I was allowed to inspect the items in this room and choose one as a gift to take home. There were jars, shoeboxes and cigar boxes filled with buttons and pearl bracelets; plastic keychain charms and gold rings; dime store toys and antique glass figurines. The walls were hung with cheap calendars and ancient oriental carpets. Feathered hats, silk dresses and ties, shoes, swords, daggers, rocks, seashells, tintype photos, leather saddlebags and ladies handbags all stuffed into trunks, chests and glass-fronted cabinets—collections of a lifetime of indiscriminate hoarding.

Aunt Evelyn greeted me as if we met every day—as if I hadn't come over two thousand miles to see her, but had just walked around the corner. We sat at her kitchen table to eat dry cookies and jasmine tea. Immediately, one of the parrots flew to her shoulder to beg for food. He sat there next to Evelyn's head—bright blue, green, red and yellow—slowly blinking his intelligent eyes and performing a slow-motion massage with his great feet.

Aunt Evelyn smiled faintly, "I'm glad you came. It's time we had a talk."

I waited.

"What do you remember of your childhood?" she asked. "Do you remember a difficult time?"

"A difficult time?"

"A time when you didn't sleep."

The hairs at the back of my head prickled and the chill travelled down my back. I shrugged at the tingle and said, "There was a time when I thought there were...people, in my room. It seems like there were nights when I didn't sleep at all— but I must have. I was afraid and mother would never come when I called out."

Aunt Evelyn nodded her head sadly. "Your mother was afraid too, and she didn't know what to do—so she did nothing. It began from the very first. You were an infant much the same as your mother was—as I was, and as your grandmother was—an infant who never cries at night and who, when her mother comes softly in to check on her, is found staring, with no frantic windmill of arms and legs, no plaintive wail—just staring. When your mother tried to gain your focused attention by looking directly in your face, you merely shifted your eyes away or closed them."

"It sounds like autism," I interrupted.

"This is not a disease."

"Oh, autism's not a disease. It's a disorder where a person—"

"It's not a disorder either. I want you to believe that."

"What is it then?"

Aunt Evelyn broke off a piece of her cookie and handed it up to the huge parrot. He took it carefully in one claw, turning it over, and slowly lifted it to the side of his beak.

"I call it—a *knowing*."

My hair crawled again.

"You will remember how you knew the very thoughts of your mother and how you became afraid—because she was?"

I nodded.

"Well, there are other things you know, but can't recognize. Your mother did not encourage you—and so you began to dream. Do you remember your very first dreams?"

I did. Very well. "They were blue," I said, "Dark blue with nothing but soft noises in them."

Aunt Evelyn nodded. "And then images began to appear—images you constructed to fill the space of your knowing and crowd it out."

I must have looked doubtful. Aunt Evelyn leaned forward and demanded, "What language do you dream in?"

How did she know?

"German," I said, "Sometimes Russian."

"And, who are the people in your dreams?"

"I don't know any of them. I've never seen them before."

"Or, perhaps you have—before."

I began to feel very uneasy and twisted my spoon in circles on the table. The great parrot squawked suddenly. Evelyn gave him another cookie.

"I don't want you to be nervous about this. I just want to talk to you about it, because it's something we have and I've always thought it should be encouraged. Your mother won't discuss it—it frightens her too much. But she has it too. And so did your grandmother—and each female before her in line according to what she told me."

"What *did* she tell you?"

"Only that as far back as can be remembered every mother's daughter has had the knowing. And she believed—as do I—that it can be developed into power, a controlled power, if it's nurtured before the child begins to dream."

I felt relieved. "If that's so, we'll never know. I'm the last daughter—and I have only sons."

Aunt Evelyn looked down into the golden-green pool of her tea cup. "That is so. And it is sad."

I reached over and put my hand on hers. "Why is it sad?" I asked. "What good is it anyway?"

She looked up then and said, "I don't know still whether it is good or bad. But I must tell you—the blue dreams come back when you're older. And I want you to be prepared. They are not what you remember. They will shake your very being!"

Aunt Evelyn was trembling. The parrot turned his head slowly toward her, but gazed sideways from one eye at me.

And I began to be afraid.

A THING OF BEAUTY

In the meadows it was common to see house cats gone wild. They would raise their heads above the tall grass, stare with uncertain eyes and dash away at the approach of man. Strange rodent creatures scurried at the slightest sound and hid under the grey moss-covered rocks. A babble of running water kept a constant background rhythm, while the tree leaves clicked together in the wind like paper tambourines. Each afternoon a soft cold rain would wet everything and settle the fine dust.

A small log house, rooted with the sage and evergreens, was surrounded by an uneven skirt of tires, motors, car bodies and assorted junk metal parts. Roscoe saved it. He saved the junk of other people, and the small recycle profited and kept him warm in the big winters. "Comes a good cold winter," he'd say, "An' we take some batteries in to sell."

But mostly, people came to Roscoe.

One stranger first came to Roscoe as a young boy. Each year after the snows melted, Ben came with his family to their vacation cabin. Drawn by the fascinating tangle of broken cars as a child, Ben was drawn to the man in his adulthood. Ambling through the broken metal, the two men often bridged the four decades between them with their common interests.

One summer Ben noticed the rusted crumbling body of an old Model-A sports coupe. It had once been painted rich dark green and tiny shreds of upholstery revealed an original tan leather.

"What an ol' beauty that one was," said Ben.

Roscoe turned fully toward Ben. He gave a half-smile and his eyes showed sudden interest. His dark wrinkles deepened for a moment around his eyes and mouth as he chuckled silently, "A thing o' beauty is a joy fo'ever."

"'Its loveliness increases; it will never pass into nothingness...'" Ben completed the quote from Keats and immediately regretted the snobbish sound.

Roscoe kicked at a stone with one cracked lace boot, cleared his throat and spat.

Ben reached his hand up to the back of his neck then shoved both hands in his pockets. "I didn't mean to sound like a smartass."

"Naw," Roscoe shook his head. "I never knew there was an endin' to it. I always just say that whenever anyone takes notice o' the ol' beauty. It makes some laugh." He turned and started toward the house. "Come on in, Vi's got coffee."

Roscoe was proud of his Indian wife, and always mentioned her blooded heritage. Vi shyly smiled and silently poured coffee. Her greying hair was braided long on each side of her head. Her house dress reached below her knees, undefined at the waist.

The two men sat on either side of the wood heater, weaving slowly in wooden rockers worn smooth on the armrests and backs from years of winter sittings. Sometimes Vi joined them, pulling up a straight-back chair from the kitchen. She sat facing the two, upright in the chair, hands in her lap. She rarely spoke, but listened attentively. *A proper Indian*, thought Ben, then mentally derided himself.

They talked of animals and their ways; and hunting, trapping, logging. They talked of machines and their ways; parts, repairs and powers. They talked of people and their ways; of survival, grief and joy. They covered a range between them, never touching a personal edge, but drawn together in their separate philosophies by a mesh of overlapping sentiment. And finally, they came to the time when they didn't talk, but sat by the fire.

One spring Ben came and Roscoe gave no welcome. He forced Ben to speak hesitant phrases through the shuttered window flung wide to admit the sun. Roscoe stood inside to one edge, mostly hidden. He was skeletal and his once tan skin was grayish. His eyes shone with over-bright fever glow.

"I don't want none to see me," Roscoe said. "You don't want to look at me. I'm all eaten up from the inside. I'll be gone by next year. There's somethin' I got to tell you. It's about my silver. I got a mine and you can have it if you work it. All you got to do is dig it out. I can't talk 'cause I get wared out, but I made you a map. Vi'll tell you where to go, an' the map'll show you from there." He thrust a wrinkled folded paper out the window.

Ben stared long at the shaking, withered hand, then quickly snatched the paper.

"Sure. Thanks, Roscoe," he said. "I'll talk to Vi about it."

"Believe me," rasped Roscoe. "You're the one should have it." He sank back, coughing.

Ben turned away. The mountain sun shone a stage-light brilliance, and he lowered his eyes as he walked slowly.

Inside his cabin he spread the map out and stared at longitude, latitude, meters, and at the big shaky "X".

It looks real, he thought. *But why didn't he use it? Maybe he thought he had more time. But when he found out he didn't, why didn't he just trust Vi to get it? She couldn't dig it herself, of course, but she could find someone who could...*

Ben looked up and blankly assessed the small room. If he did get some silver out, how much was it? Would it be worth digging for?

"That's stupid," he said aloud, and thought: *What do I know about mining?* Then, ashamed at his mind's greedy turn, he remembered Roscoe's wasted form and fell into a self-indulgent reverie.

A knock at the door startled him. He crossed to the door in three paces, glad of the diversion. Vi stood at the step, holding a cloth-wrapped bundle. She looked at Ben for a long minute, then decided he wouldn't speak first. "I've come to talk," she said.

Still surprised, Ben nodded and motioned her in. They stood uncertain for a moment, then both scraped chairs out from the small kitchen table and sat. Suddenly embarrassed before Vi's stolid face, Ben began, "I'm sorry about Roscoe."

Vi looked down at her hands and the cloth package now resting in her lap. The movement was uneasy, but she didn't fidget. Looking up quickly, she said, "I feel sorry too, that's why I come. You've talked to Roscoe some, and you know him some. I want to tell you what you might oughta know—what I want you to know."

Vi lifted the cloth package to the table and slowly unlapped four corners. Against the rough cloth the large rock looked like an enormous uncut gemstone. The mass of it was clear green-blue, streaked in sparkling silver-white jagged veins.

"Then it's true?" asked Ben as he lifted his eyes from the rock to Vi.

"Part," said Vi. She shifted very slightly and began. "Roscoe's had nothin', no things. Roscoe had two sons. They had no want to work nor go for schoolin', nor even to minin'. They did like the junk, though. They scavenged and brought back ever' bit. Only they begun to bring home whole cars that was abandoned on the roads—even though they still belonged to somebody. Seemed like they couldn't stop, and now, they're in prison."

"So that's why he asked me?" Ben felt exhilarated.

"Part," said Vi, and continued. "Roscoe met me when he's rodeoin'. I still lived on the reservation then, still with my momma. I came in to the rodeo, Roscoe saw me and met me, and begun comin' to visit at the reservation. When it looked serious, I said I'd marry if he quit the rodeoin'. So he gave his two horses to my family, as honor to their ways, and to me he gave this silver. I came with him as wife and we had lots of hard times, but I always kept my marriage gift. Roscoe would want to sell it, and I'd say no. He thought it was woman's want for fine things, but he never knew it meant more than a pretty rock."

"A thing of beauty...," mumbled Ben; then quickly asked, "Why didn't he just go get some more?"

Vi gave a faint longing half-smile. "He couldn't. The mine is on Indian land. It belongs to my tribe. It's not his claim."

"But," Ben felt somehow betrayed, "he wanted to try to get it?"

Vi looked straight at Ben. "He thought to get you to do it—for me. He meant no bad thing. He don't remember it's mine already."

"No," Ben agreed.

Vi rose wearily. Slowly she wrapped the stone and lifted it to the door. "I'll be goin'."

Ben nodded, then walked to the door and watched her walk through the evening. Her skirt caught at the sagebrush, startling a wild cat. It raised its head above the tall grass, stared for a moment with uncertain eyes. Ben closed the door and automatically began to build up the woodfire in the evening chill. He sat silent and watched the flames rise. Slowly, he fed the map into the fire and watched it burn black and thought of the life that was curling and shrinking.

MEET THE AUTHOR

For 25 years Debra Litton taught gifted students, grades 7 through 12, often discussing the themes of honor, love, hate, revenge, and prejudice that are reflected in her writing. Now retired, she lives with her husband in Lawrence, Kansas, and enjoys gardening, reading, and her cat Umi.

Curious about other Crossroad Press books? Stop by our website:
http://crossroadpress.com
We offer quality writing
in digital, audio, and print formats.

Subscribe to our newsletter on the website homepage and receive a
free eBook.

www.ingramcontent.com/pod-product-compliance
Lightning Source LLC
Chambersburg PA
CBHW022019170626
46808CB00003B/979